BEAUTIFULLY PAINTED

CANDIED CRUSH #6

CHARITY PARKERSON

—Warning: This book is intended for readers over the age of 18.

Two people from opposite sides of the tracks. A love they can't shake. They are a mistake neither of them can stop making.

As a teenager, Dawson was fostered by Milo's family. While everyone had been trying to force them to be brothers, they had been falling in love. That love cost Dawson everything. Now, even though he knows he has to forget Milo, he doesn't know how. Not that it matters. They can never be together again. Dawson must leave him behind.

Once upon a time, Milo ruined Dawson's life. At the time, he had big plans to make everything right. Unfortunately, Dawson never gave him a chance to try. Now they spend all their time dancing around each other and making each other miserable. It's a situation Milo no longer knows how to fix.

Then fate shows Milo an opening. He has to take it no matter the cost. All Milo can do is hope Dawson doesn't end up hating him even more than he already does. Everything rides on this last-ditch effort to win Dawson for good. Otherwise, they'll both lose.

ONE

SILVER EYES FOLLOWED his every move. The same hungry gaze every day while Dawson worked, waiting tables at The Back Porch. Dawson never tired of it. Milo MacDermott's open stalking was the only reason Dawson still got up every morning. He loved Milo's shaggy and ink-colored hair and the tiny diamond in his nose. The way he looked innocent yet wicked at the same time. Dawson loved Milo. Things should be that simple. They were in love and that should be that. Happily ever after. Except it wasn't that cut and dry. There was nothing uncomplicated about them. In fact, there was no line between love and hate when it came to Milo. His feelings for Milo were in a huge vat, mixing hatred, love, lust, and longing together every second of the day. Sometimes, he thought he might go insane.

"You look gorgeous today."

Dawson's gaze slid Milo's way at the quietly spoken words as he passed Milo's table. He didn't respond. Dawson couldn't. The heat blasting at him from Milo's stare stole his voice. No one understood. Milo had one of those voices. It was soulful and caressed the skin. His stare pierced the ice surrounding Dawson's heart. It was like a whole magical world lived inside Milo. He was creative and insightful. Everything he did amazed Dawson and made him proud. He made Dawson wish he had a tenth of Milo's talent. Milo was a painter and a poet. He gave life to beautiful things. Dawson was no one.

He turned away.

"Could I speak to your manager? I've been waiting entirely too long for my order. Some of us have to work."

Dawson bit back an inner sigh. He needed this job. His position at the popular coffeehouse was the only thing standing between him and homelessness. "I am the manager and I have your coffee right here." Dawson tried to stay calm as he set a glass mug on the table in front of his irate customer. It wasn't someone he had seen before. The guy had diva

2

written all over him, but this was Dawson's life. He took abuse from customers and got lousy tips.

"That's not what I ordered."

Dawson took a deep breath and counted to three inside his head. "That's a white geisha, which is what you ordered."

The guy practically vibrated with open rage. His perfectly styled dark hair didn't budge as he shook his head. "No. It isn't. White geishas are white. This is brown. You can keep this cheap knock-off shit."

In an instant, hot coffee arched through the air as a cup flew Dawson's way. Dawson jumped back, trying to avoid getting hit by the scalding brew. He only half succeeded. The dark liquid soaked his shirt but missed his face. Luckily, he grabbed the hem of his shirt and pulled the material away from his skin fast enough to save himself from any actual damage. There was only a mild stinging on his skin.

"It's time for you to go." The softly spoken rage was as familiar as his own voice. Dawson didn't have to look Milo's way to know his silver eyes flashed with fury. Milo always looked at him with one of three expressions: longing, confusion, or pure anger. Dawson had all three expressions memorized.

"I'm not going any fucking where. This is a free country and I want the right order."

A third voice joined the argument while Dawson still tried to wrap his mind around having hot coffee tossed his way. "Throwing a scalding hot beverage at someone is assault. I can arrest you or you can leave. Those are your options."

Dawson looked the new arrival's way. Valor, a regular at The Back Porch who was also Dawson's friend and landlord, was in uniform and looked serious, cutting through Dawson's shock. His hand rested on the cuffs on his side—like he fully intended to enforce his threat. Valor's gaze slid his way. He tilted his head toward the back. "Go take a second. I've got this and this place can run without you while you take a breath."

With a nod, Dawson took a step back. As always, his gaze found Milo. Milo stood over Dawson's attacker with his arms crossed over his chest—like he physically held himself back. His hard gaze stayed locked on the coffee flinger, leaving no doubt he planned to kill him if he made the wrong move. Dawson turned away and headed for the kitchen. There were extra shirts in the storeroom. His heartbeat sounded loud inside his ears. Dawson's hands shook as he wet a washcloth at the sink and tried wiping away the mess. Every day was a unique challenge, but this was new. Dawson was so exhausted. No one told people how much they would struggle through adulthood. Dawson's dad had died when Dawson had been sixteen. Since he had no other family that wanted him, he had been alone in the world. With no money for college, and no actual skills after high school, here he was, managing a coffeehouse. The money wasn't the worst, but L.A. had ridiculous rent. Living here cost way more than Dawson could afford. Some days, like today, Dawson wanted to give up. He was tired. Everything sucked and hurt. This wasn't the future he had expected. For one thing, he didn't have Milo. Every day, that was a huge loss.

Dawson headed into the bathroom to change. As he turned on the light, his reflection caught his attention. There were black smudges beneath each of his dead-looking eyes. If Dawson didn't know his age, he would guess forty rather than twenty-two. Life had been kicking his ass the last few... his whole goddamn life, actually.

Dawson took a deep breath and then another. The sound of his breathing, as he tried to find peace, had a memory firing to life in his head. His eyes fell closed.

"What in the hell are you doing?"

Milo's eyes stayed shut. His hands rested on his

knees, palms up, and he sat cross-legged on the floor. With his spine arrow straight, Milo took another visibly deep breath before answering. "Meditating."

"Jesus. Your entire family is like some new age hipster dumpster fire."

A slight smile touched Milo's lips. One silver eye opened and focused on Dawson. "Are you man enough to try something new, or is bashing everything you don't understand your way of pussying out?"

Fuck that. Dawson was no pussy. He sat across from Milo, matching his pose. Milo's lips twitched for a moment, but he didn't laugh. Instead, he gave Dawson a sharp nod and went back to breathing.

"What am I supposed to be doing here?"

"Close your eyes," Milo said, sounding calm. "Don't try to control your breathing. Just focus on the process. The way the body moves as you inhale and exhale." With his eyes closed, Dawson concentrated on the sound of Milo's voice as Milo kept up the instructions. "Find one thing in your mind to focus on and let everything else go. Don't think about anything else. Let the day slip away. All your stresses. Just find one calming object and breathe. Stretch out your shoulders and your back. Feel yourself sinking deeper into relaxation."

Dawson took a deep breath.

Milo touched Dawson's chest.

Dawson's eyes flew open. Milo was so close, Dawson could smell his cologne.

He shook his head at Dawson. "Don't look at me. Close your eyes."

Dawson did as bade.

Milo didn't move away. His fingers didn't lift from Dawson's chest. "Breathe from here. Focus on the way the air moves through your lungs. I promise you'll feel better when we're done here." Milo's lips touched his.

Dawson sucked in a sharp breath at the contact and he backed away. His eyes shot open.

A wicked look crossed Milo's features. "Did the meditation work or do you plan to hit me now?"

"Let me see." Dawson's eyes opened as Milo tugged at his shirt and pulled him from the past. "Did he burn you? Do I need to take you to the ER?"

With his memories still crippling him, Dawson stood still while Milo peeled his shirt off. "No. I'm okay. He scalded me a little but not enough to hurt me."

"Fucking bastard. If he ever shows his face around here again, no one will ever find his body."

Dawson couldn't look away from the rage flashing in Milo's eyes as Milo inspected Dawson's stomach, looking for injuries. "I guess all that new age hippie meditation isn't working for you anymore."

The rage bled from Milo's eyes. A smile touched his lips. "You know I've never been able to tolerate seeing you hurt." His gaze moved down Dawson's bare torso again and froze on his chest. Dawson had forgotten about the tattoo his friend Dean had recently done for him. It was too late to cover it up. Milo's hand slowly rose. He lightly traced the words permanently etched on Dawson's skin. Milo's chest rose and fell as a ragged-sounding breath escaped him. He took a step closer to Dawson, making the tiny bathroom seem even smaller. His lips lightly brushed the tattoo before moving to Dawson's neck. Dawson gripped the edge of the sink and held on, trying desperately to cling to sanity. He wanted to cry and scream. Dawson wanted to haul Milo closer and have his way. The only thing Dawson didn't want was to push Milo away, but that was what he did, because this was a waste of time. Dawson couldn't ruin Milo's life.

"Thank you for checking on me."

Hurt flashed in Milo's eyes, making Dawson wish for the millionth time things were different. Milo visibly swallowed—like his throat hurt. He didn't quite meet Dawson's stare. "As long as you're okay..." Milo walked away, as if he lost the ability to try any longer mid speech. Dawson got it. He really did. Milo had fought for him much longer than Dawson ever dreamed he would. Much longer than anyone else would have fought. He had always known the day would eventually come when he pushed Milo too far. Maybe today was that day.

———

THIS WAS A MISTAKE.

As Milo had traced the words of Dawson's tattoo with the tip of his finger, he had been transported back in time for a moment. Back to when they had been different people and Dawson had written those words to Milo before skipping out on him for good. The thing was, even though Milo had tossed that letter back in Dawson's face the very next day, they were a mistake. The words weren't a lie. Dawson and Milo were one gigantic anomaly casting ripples through the lives of everyone around them, disrupting nature. They were a taboo topic. They were the gossip Milo's family whispered about at gatherings. Milo always caught the same bits and pieces when people spoke of them behind their hands. They were shameful. How long had this been going on? Someone should do something. Say something. It was all so... stupid.

Milo had been twelve and Dawson had been thirteen when Milo's mom had hired Dawson's dad as a live-in bodyguard. That meant the single father had brought his son to live under Milo's roof when he moved in. As kids from opposite sides of the tracks, they had hated each other on sight. While Milo had always been a sensitive soul, learning piano, art, and reading his precious collection of classic novels, Dawson had been the athlete. Being raised by a single father meant Dawson had started with tee-ball and touch football before growing with each sport. Milo had been tiny. Dawson had looked huge to him. They had nothing in common and were suddenly thrust together. Milo thought he had fallen into a nightmare.

Then, shortly after Dawson's sixteenth birthday, his father had a massive heart attack. Everything between them changed. With nowhere else to go, Milo's mom took charge of Dawson, fostering him. Milo and Dawson found themselves in the oddest place. Everyone tried forcing them to act as real brothers. They weren't and never could be, but they were the only ones who knew why. It was a situation that worsened every day until Milo learned his mom intended to adopt Dawson before he turned eighteen. Milo had been forced to extremes to stop her. In his exuberance and ignorant youth, he had ended up ruining Dawson's life instead. Now Dawson worked at The Back Porch, barely scraping by. Milo couldn't forgive himself. Dawson couldn't forgive him either. Milo didn't know how to get back to the nights when they had sneaked into each other's rooms. The stolen touches. The whispered words of love. Milo's gut twisted with longing. Maybe they had been stupid and reckless teenagers, but their love hadn't died, even after Milo ruined them. Dawson was twenty-two and Milo was twenty-one now. There was nothing standing between them but Dawson's anger.

As Milo slipped back inside the dining room of the coffee shop, leaving Dawson behind, he swore all eyes turned his way. Knowing stares followed him to the door. It was possible more stood between them than anger and guilt. Milo wouldn't give up, though. He understood he was young and had a famous mother. Milo had his whole life ahead of him and could probably have anyone he set his mind on, but his heart had been stolen at fifteen when he had stolen a kiss from a hurting boy. Milo had never been flighty. He might be a dreamer, but he was a loyal one. Dawson belonged to him. Milo wouldn't stop coming back until Dawson gave in for good or they both died of old age. Maybe even then, Milo would chase him into the next life. He didn't know how to stop. Loving Dawson was all he knew.

With his bottom lip held between his teeth, Milo watched as Dawson threw the football as hard as he could, sending everyone on the field scrambling. He was getting better at remembering all the plays. Milo didn't really care about football, but Dawson did. That was all that mattered.

"You shouldn't stare at Dawson like that. You'll have everyone thinking he's like you. Plus, aren't you two brothers or something?"

Milo sat on his hands to keep from showing the way they automatically shook. He hated confrontation, but it seemed like every single one of Dawson's friends loved to start shit.

"We're not brothers. What do you mean people will think he's like me?"

The red-haired teenage boy who started this horrible conversation didn't back down. In fact, he smirked, as if relishing an upcoming moment of cruelty. "You know, gay. Everyone knows you like to suck dick."

"*Whoa. Did you just say everyone knows you like to suck dick?*"

Milo dropped his chin to hide his smile as Dawson appeared from nowhere at just the right moment to save him.

"*No. Milo here—*"

"*Damn, Caine. There's nothing wrong with being gay, but straight up bragging that you like sucking dick is a bit much, don't you think? Show some class, dude.*"

Dawson's smile made him impossible to resist. Milo couldn't look away from him. Dawson's sweet brown gaze slid his way. He winked. "Don't let this guy lure you into his big white van. You're my ride home."

Milo fought the urge to smile like an idiot. "Don't worry. I can't be lured away. I've had my dick sucked by better."

Dawson threw his head back and roared with laughter. Milo tried to look away, but he couldn't. Caine was right. Anyone could look at Milo and see Milo's desire. There was no one else out there for Milo. Dawson had been his first real crush. That small torch had since turned into an inferno. No one else would do. Milo's smile dimmed. No one else could know. If anyone learned about what they did when they were alone, they would take Dawson away from him. That wasn't an option. Milo would die without him.

He would definitely chase him into the next life.

WITH HIS HEART still in his throat, Dawson made his way back to the dining area. He probably had twelve more customers ready to toss some coffee his way after being kept waiting. Plus, he had a mess to clean up. As Dawson cleared the door between the kitchen and dining room, his steps slowed. Everything was fine. The broken mug and puddle of coffee had been cleared away. No one yelled for service and it was all thanks to Valor. The muscular cop looked out of place, moving from table to table, checking on people while still carrying a broom.

With a shake of his head, Dawson moved to relieve him. "Thank you. I'll take this."

Valor held tight to the broom. "I've got it. You should head on home. I gave Wrecker a call. He's on his way, so everything is under control here."

Dawson tried clinging to his smile, but he couldn't. He didn't do this job for the fun of it.

Dawson needed the money. "Thank you, but I can't afford to go home."

A sweet smile touched Valor's lips. "As your landlord, I'm knocking a hundred dollars off your rent this month. Go home. I think you need a mental health day."

Without warning, Dawson's eyes started burning. He felt like everyone's charity case. He was angry and hurt. Dawson wanted to find the guy who had tossed coffee his way and put a fist in his face. He wanted to chase Milo and wipe away years of damage they caused each other. Dawson wanted to climb on top of a table and scream at the top of his lungs that he loved and hated everyone under this roof. Goddamn it. He needed a mental health day. Still, he argued. "You already do too much for me. I know you're already charging me way less for that apartment than you could get from someone else. I can't take any more advantage of you than I already am."

A sexy-sounding rumble of laughter came from deep inside Valor's chest. "No one takes advantage of me. I'm a hardcore top. I do all the taking."

A snort escaped Dawson before he could stop it. "Thank god there isn't a partner who has to put up with you all day."

"You're just the lucky one who pulled the short straw. You get to put up with the weird me. Don't change the subject. You're going home."

Dawson took a deep breath. He knew Valor was right. When a day started this bad, it was time to walk away and hope for a better tomorrow. "All right. When Wrecker gets here, I'll go."

"Nope." Valor set the broom aside and spun Dawson toward the door. With his hands on his shoulders, Valor marched him out. "Whatever tips you've made this morning, I'll bring by this evening when I get home. I've got things under control."

"Fine." Dawson tried not to drag his feet like a child. He recognized that Valor was being a good friend. "I'm going. I'm going. Sheesh."

As they cleared the door, Valor kissed his cheek. "Get lost, babe. You deserve the break."

Before Dawson could thank him again, Valor disappeared back inside. Dawson didn't know what he would do without the middle-aged Hawaiian cop who had taken him in when the rest of the world had turned their back on him. Valor had found Dawson walking down the road a month before his eighteenth birthday. Instead of forcing him into a foster home or taking him back to Milo's mom, Rachel, Valor had taken him home. Working together, they had converted Valor's detached garage into a studio apartment. The labor Dawson put into the place paid his rent for six months until Dawson could find a job. Between Valor and a twenty-thousand-dollar policy from his dad's death that came to him at eighteen, Dawson had survived. He had bought a cheap car and some extra groceries. That was all it took to wipe out that money.

Since Dawson didn't know how to do anything and he sure as hell couldn't afford any type of secondary education, he was stuck. Luckily, Valor didn't seem to be in any hurry to get rid of him. Still, Dawson never forgot that he was on borrowed time. Eventually, he would have to get out of Valor's hair. For Dawson, that would mean leaving L.A., and—most likely—California. He couldn't afford to consider staying.

As Dawson drove home, he thought about all the research he had been doing into other states. So far, Nevada looked to be his best bet. Between Milo occasionally giving him money for paintings he sold of Dawson's image and working nonstop for Wrecker, Dawson had a little money saved. In fact, if he left before Monday—when the rent was due next —he would probably have enough to make the move now. He was off for the next two days and now he was off today too. If he started driving right this minute, he could be in Nevada by this afternoon. It was the perfect time to head up that way, look for a job, and eyeball some potential apartments.

There was a hole aching in Dawson's heart just thinking about leaving Milo behind. The thing was, he should have left a long time ago. As soon as he had gotten that twenty grand from his dad's death, Dawson should have split. Dawson hadn't done Milo any favors by hanging around, except he had thought they would be together. From the bottom of his soul, Dawson had believed that would be their future.

Milo had shown at the hotel they had agreed upon. Dawson had known he would. It had been hell waiting six months for Milo to turn eighteen, but when midnight struck and Milo became a legal adult, he had turned up at the motel where they had sworn to meet—like he couldn't wait another second to be with Dawson. Dawson knew the feeling. Every day, since the day Milo's mom had tossed him out, Dawson had died a little more without Milo. He had been used to Milo sneaking into his bed every night when they had been under the same roof. Now, the nights were long and empty. Dawson wasn't dumb. He knew they were young, and people thought they were irrational, but Dawson knew his heart. He loved Milo, and Milo loved him. That was why they had to disappear. Dawson plotted while Milo slept. He had managed to hold on to the money he gotten from his dad's life insurance for five months now. Milo had a car. Between the two of them, they could make it.

Dawson's cellphone rang. He rushed to answer, hoping not to wake Milo. "Hello?"

"Is he with you?"

Dawson's eyes fell closed as Rachel's voice cut through the line. He stepped outside so Milo wouldn't hear. "Yeah. He's here."

Silence met his response. After a moment, Rachel cleared her throat. "I'd threaten to ruin your life, but I doubt you'd budge."

Even though Milo's mom couldn't see him, Dawson shrugged. "You already took everything from me."

"So you decided to steal my son? Is this some type of sick revenge?"

In the face of her obvious hysterics, Dawson tried to stay calm. "I'm not stealing him. He loves me and I love him. He came to me willingly."

"Then I suggest you find a way to make him come home just as willingly."

"Or what?" Dawson truly didn't want to incite Rachel's rage. She just had genuinely already taken all there was to take from him. He didn't know what else she thought she could do.

"It's you or me. If he wants to stay with you, I can't stop him, but you're taking him with nothing. I'll empty his bank account and report his car stolen. Mark my words, he'll resent you when he's slaving away at a forty-hour a week job while scraping pennies together and watching his love for art die. Do you really want to kill the thing you love? Because that's what will happen if you take him away from everything he knows. Milo has never had to work. He's been allowed to see the beauty in life, creating art and poetry. If you're willing to steal that from him, can you really say you love him?"

Dawson ended the call and turned his phone off for good measure. As he slipped back inside the room, Milo rolled onto his back. Dawson set the phone aside before moving to sit at Milo's hip. For what felt like hours, Dawson watched Milo sleep. He knew Rachel wasn't bluffing. After all, she had claimed to love him as a son, but tossed him out with nothing when she caught Milo and Dawson making out. He would like to think she would never do such a thing to her own blood, but Dawson couldn't risk it. Milo's ability to see the beauty in everything, including Dawson, was the reason Dawson had fallen in love with him. If

Rachel cut Milo from her life and purse strings, he would be forced to live as Dawson had for the past six months. Milo wasn't hard like Dawson. He couldn't mop floors and scrub public restrooms. Dawson would have to watch the wonder slowly die in Milo's eyes. He couldn't do it.

Dawson stood and gathered his things. He found a hotel scratchpad and pen. For a moment, the pen hovered over the paper. He didn't know what to say. Milo was loyal. Dawson wasn't sure there was anything he could say that would make Milo stay away. The truth definitely wouldn't cut it. He already knew Milo would claim not to care about the money, but that was only because he didn't understand the reality of living without it. In the end, Dawson kept it simple. His heart couldn't take much more.

He set the note on top of Milo's phone. His words stared up at him.

This was a mistake.

It was the biggest lie Dawson had ever told in his life. For a long time, he had carried those words around in his pocket after Milo turned up on his doorstep the next morning and tossed the note in Dawson's face. Sometimes, he would take them out and stare at them, while wondering if there was anything else he could have done. But then, he would think about all the times he had watched Milo take the stage and spout the most beautiful poetry he had ever heard, and he would refold the note and put it back in his wallet. Eventually, after becoming friends with a tattoo artist, Dawson had gotten the words permanently etched on his chest. Right next to his heart. They were his everyday reminder of why he couldn't be with the only person he loved. It hadn't been a mistake leaving Milo. He loved Milo enough to want him to have a wonderful life. The real mistake was Dawson's existence. Without him, Milo would be free. Someone could keep Milo warm every night without being an embarrassment. It was well past time for Dawson to let Milo go. It was time for him to leave. His time with Milo was over.

TWO

DAWSON STILL WORE his black suit. Milo hadn't been allowed to go to the funeral. In fact, when he had suggested they should go for appearances sake, hoping to use an argument his mom would understand, she had only snorted. All day, Milo had pictured Dawson alone at a graveside somewhere. Milo's mom had made sure Dawson had been chauffeured there. He had left alone and come back the same way. Milo's heart broke for Dawson, but he didn't know what to say.

Milo moved to sit next to him on the front steps. As usual, Dawson didn't acknowledge his presence. Milo was used to being ignored. At least Dawson's silence didn't feel empty. When everyone else in the house pretended he wasn't there—his mom included—

it didn't feel like they were play acting. They truly didn't see him. Milo was certain he was no more than a ghost, completely invisible to the human eye. Dawson never made him feel alone. It was more like Dawson never knew what to say to Milo. That was fine. Milo never knew what to say either, but he tried today.

"I'm sorry about your dad. He was nice. I liked him."

Dawson didn't look his way, but he gave a subtle nod that he had heard.

Milo couldn't stop staring at his profile. Dawson's eyes were red-rimmed and swollen. A muscle in his jaw flexed, making Milo wonder if he would fall apart. Milo would be here if it happened.

"I tried to get Mom to let me go with you, but she blew me off. I hope you weren't alone there."

Even though Dawson still didn't speak, he reached over and took Dawson's hand. Milo's gaze dropped to their linked fingers. No one ever touched him. Before he could stop himself, Milo covered their clasped hands with his other hand, holding on tight. In an instant, he was terrified Dawson would let go and he would never feel human touch again. Dawson didn't pull away and Milo vowed to stay put for as long as Dawson did. He would sit at Dawson's side *for the rest of his life if Dawson didn't let go. Milo would give him peace.*

THE SMALL CROWD went silent as Milo moved to stand behind the microphone. His gaze swept over the audience before landing on a surprising new face. Milo liked these small affairs at the local library. They were held after hours and Milo never knew anyone there other than the librarians that kept inviting back. Seeing Valor Kamaka in the crowd almost shocked Milo into forgetting his lines. He found his center again and dove in.

"I made a million mistakes, but you weren't one. I told a million lies, but never to you. I gave away everything, so we would match. No one tells you that you can never go back." Milo poured his heart into the speaking poetry he adored. These nights were his therapy sessions. His audience was his psychiatrist. He let his wounds bleed onto the crowd, releasing some of the pain that kept him crippled all hours of the day. Sometimes, for just a moment, after he left these events, he thought he might survive. Milo would go home and pour the rest of his energy into his paintings. Art was all he had these days. All that sustained him. Milo was more than aware this might always be his only love until he breathed his last. Some people simply weren't meant to fall asleep beside anyone.

By the time his final words died, Milo noticed a few people swiping at their eyes, but he felt empty. He stepped off the stage, doing his best to find a smile as he spoke to each person who stopped him. Milo had become so lost in his pain that he forgot Valor was there until they stood toe to toe.

"Is everything you write about Dawson?"

"Yes." Milo saw no reason to lie. He wasn't ashamed.

"Do you mind if we get a coffee and talk?"

Milo shrugged. "I have nothing else going on and you came all this way."

Side by side, they headed out. Without discussing where they would go, they headed toward a nearby donut shop—like they had planned ahead. Milo wanted to ask how Valor had found him, but he didn't. If Valor had sought him out, then this was about Dawson. Milo didn't need to know anything else.

Valor held the door open for Milo—like a gentleman. With a small smile of thanks, Milo headed inside and chose a booth by the window.

Valor slid in across from him and Milo had to stop himself from shifting nervously. Valor was old enough to be his father. Since Milo had never had one of those, the closest thing he could equate Valor to was Dawson's dad, Trevor. Trevor had always made Milo nervous. He had been too big, taking up too much space. Valor reminded Milo a lot of him. That thought made him smile. Trevor had been kind.

"Did you have a topic to discuss or did you just need a partner in crime for getting coffee at eight o'clock at night an hour and a half from home?"

Valor chuckled. "Both, I suppose. I've always heard that you're an amazing speaking poet, but I had no idea. You're very good."

Milo swiped his palms on his thighs. "Thank you. I usually do the open mic night at The Back Porch. You could have seen me there at any time."

"Do you mind if I ask what happened between Dawson and you?"

A bright smile snapped to Milo's lips at the sudden question. It was pure self-preservation. "What? Are you saying you really haven't heard the greatest gossip around?"

Valor shook his head. "Dawson's dad had just died, and he was kind of broken when I took him in. I didn't want to push too hard. Over the years, he's

27

stayed pretty tight-lipped about you and I don't have time for gossip. All I know is that he's in love with you, and it's obvious the feeling is mutual. For whatever reason, you two just lash each other against the rocks nonstop. I need to know why."

"Dawson's dad died almost two years before you took him in. I'm the reason he was broken when you found him." A sad smile pulled at Milo's lips. It felt almost cathartic to make the admission. "My mom is Rachel MacDermott."

Valor's eyebrows shot to his hairline. "The Rachel MacDermott? The famous actress?"

Milo nodded. "Don't sound so thrilled. She's really not that great of a human. Anyhow," Milo said, diving in with both feet. "She picked up a nasty stalker when I was twelve and she decided she needed a full-time live-in bodyguard. Dawson's dad, Trevor, was her favorite choice, even though he wasn't ideal, because he came with a son. Really, though, it wasn't that big of a deal for her. After all, nannies had been raising her son until I had gotten old enough to be completely ignored. She expected Trevor's son would be no different—out of sight, out of mind—and we were left on our own." A smile tugged at Milo's lips. He could still picture the first time he met Dawson.

"I've always been small," Milo admitted as he fell into the memory of those days. "Dawson is only five

+ months older than me, so I was extremely shocked to meet this huge kid who would be living under my roof. I didn't like him and tried to steer clear, but I was also kind of fascinated. He was so different from me. Dawson played every sport and I practiced all the arts. There was no middle ground. We were chauffeured to school and back together and that was the extent of the time we spent in each other's company. Our friends were not the same. We ignored each other at all costs."

Milo took a breath, as all the feelings overwhelmed him. "Then, Trevor died. My mom jumped in like people would scorn her if she pretended to be anything less than charitable. Dawson had nowhere to go. If she turned him out, people would talk. So she made all the proper noises and kept him, telling everyone how she loved him as a son and couldn't possibly let him go. Everyone started referring to us as brothers and Dawson just turned quieter and became less every day. The smaller he got, the more I gravitated toward him."

"What can I get you guys?"

"Two black coffees," Valor said, answering the

waiter for the both of them without ever taking his gaze from Milo.

Milo realized Valor cared. He truly wanted to know what happened to them. Milo went from telling the story to his hands to holding Valor's stare. "He would sit alone at lunch and I would sit with him. We didn't talk, but I was there. The more time I spent with him, the more he fascinated me. I wanted to hear his thoughts. Watch him grow and get better. I wanted the old Dawson back, even if it meant he went back to ignoring me. Then, one day, he sought me out." A smile tugged at Milo's lips. He fought the urge to cover his face at the memory of stealing a kiss while teaching Dawson how to meditate.

Milo shook his head, shaking off his embarrassment, but he couldn't make his smile budge. "We started doing everything together. If I had piano lessons, he went. If he had football practice, I was there. He stopped talking to everyone but me, and I did the same." Milo shrugged. "I don't know when it happened or why, but we just fell in love." Milo's smile slipped away. "Then my mom decided she would adopt Dawson before he turned eighteen so he would be a real member of the family."

Valor sucked in a hiss, reminding Milo he wasn't alone.

Milo nodded. "Exactly. I couldn't let that happen. Maybe I sound dramatic, but I felt like my entire existence depended upon that not happening." Milo swallowed past the lump growing in his throat. "So I teased and lured Dawson into the theater room, where things turned heated. I got Dawson out of most of his clothes, knowing my mom was headed in there any moment. She busted us, just like I knew she would." For a moment, Milo turned inside himself. He hated the way he felt about that day, because he was torn. "I saved us and ruined Dawson's life all in one huge moment of panic. The idea of people finding out I had been having sex with a boy she had been telling people would be her new son totally outweighed what people would think if she put Dawson out into the street. I don't know what I thought she would do. It never occurred to me that she couldn't adopt Dawson without his permission. I wasn't thinking at all. All I knew was I didn't want to lose Dawson, and then I not only lost him, but I took a sledgehammer to his life."

Milo blinked back tears. "If you hadn't found him that day, I don't know what would've happened to him. Thank you for taking him in. I've never said that, but you've never really spoken to me, so..." Milo sucked in a deep breath. "I used to worry he would fall in love with you and forget about me." Even Milo didn't understand why he had confessed that. The words sounded shaky even to his ears. "Sorry. Everyone I grew up with and my entire family considers Dawson my brother. No one really understands that he was never that to me. I'm pretty used to getting judged over this."

Valor nodded. Two cups of coffee arrived, and they doctored their drinks in silence. Milo felt drained. In truth, he was always exhausted from trying to claw his way back to Dawson.

"You probably don't want to hear another opinion on this," Valor said suddenly, as if he had been questioning whether he should speak at all.

Milo shrugged. "Go for it. I can't imagine it's anything I haven't heard before."

Valor sipped his coffee and eyed Milo over the edge. His dark eyes looked kind and wise. Milo decided he was a little interested to hear his thoughts. Valor set his cup aside. "I think your mom played you."

Milo blinked. He hadn't expected that one. "Okay. I take it back. This isn't an opinion I've heard before."

A deep-sounding chuckle rumbled from Valor. "I know you're grown, but you haven't been around as long as I have. Your story was very telling, but I don't think you realize how much. I think, and I could be wrong, but I don't believe I am, I think your mom isn't blind. She saw you falling for a boy she considers beneath you, and—being an adult—she knew you would rebel if she said anything. So, instead, she decided to start treating you like brothers, hoping to shut things down. When that didn't stop the way you looked at him, she decided to make you brothers for real."

Milo sipped his coffee and tried not to react. A thousand memories flared to life. Times when he thought his mom knew more than she let on. Not that any of that mattered any longer. "I guess the whys and hows don't really matter anymore. The results were the same. Dawson hates me and I have done absolutely everything I can think to do to change that. Occasionally, he'll give me just enough to keep me hanging on, but then he pulls away again. I'm not going anywhere, though. I'm not giving up."

Valor nodded. "That's good, because I think he bailed."

Milo blinked. Valor's tone and expression hadn't

wavered from conversational, but his words didn't match. "What do you mean, bailed?"

Valor made a dismissive motion. "Like, took off. I popped in to give him his tips from this morning, since I made him leave work after the coffee incident, and he was gone. Normally, I wouldn't think anything about it, but it looks like he took a lot of his things with him."

For a moment, Milo couldn't react. Everything inside him went still before a smile exploded across his lips.

Valor's eyebrows rose at Milo's reaction. "This makes you... happy."

Milo nodded. "He's running."

Valor's confusion visibly grew by the second. He blinked and looked around, as if grasping at straws. "Why is that a good thing?"

Milo shot to his feet and dug out his wallet. He answered while dropping a few bills on the table. "He wants me to chase him, even if he doesn't know it yet. Years ago, we talked about running away and made a plan." Milo couldn't stop smiling. "He's finally running, and I know exactly how to find him." Milo barely stopped himself from dancing in place. "I have to go." He needed to get his shit and get moving. Dawson had a head start. Milo couldn't get to him fast enough.

Valor set his hand on Milo's arm, snapping him back to reality. He focused on Valor's dark eyes as the man spoke, and he knew Valor cared. "Let him know his apartment will always be waiting, for you both if you need it."

On impulse, Milo hugged Valor. "Thank you. I'll have him call you."

"Wait," Valor said, stopping Milo again as he tried to get away. He handed Milo a card. "Call me if you need me. I'll be there."

Milo tightened his grip on the square of paper. He was more grateful than Valor could know. "I will. Thanks again." Milo rushed away before Valor could stop him again. There was no time to lose. He had a million things to do and his patience was thin. Dawson was out there somewhere, waiting, even if he didn't know it yet. Milo would make everything better. The time had finally come.

NEVADA HAD Dawson hitting a lot of dead ends. Most of the apartments he visited were either already closed to tours for the night or didn't have any studio apartments open. All Dawson could do was start again tomorrow. The motel he had chosen for the night wasn't bad for the price. He actually found a place with a pyramid and a casino for only thirty dollars a night. Dawson hadn't known anyone was that cheap anymore. Between that and low gas prices, he didn't feel too bad about the impromptu trip. In fact, despite not having any luck finding an apartment, he felt pretty good about the town. Dawson needed a fresh start. Enterprise, Nevada seemed like as good a place as any.

Dawson pulled out his phone and texted Milo, the way he did every night. He told Milo everything he had done today and how much he loved and missed him before erasing the entire text, just as he did every night.

A knock sounded, confusing the hell out of Dawson. He headed for the door and checked the peephole. A chuckle rose in his throat as he opened the door. "You're like a magician. How do you always find me?"

Milo's bright smile always stopped any hint of irritation. Not to mention, Milo's was the only face he ever wanted to see. "I have a GPS tag on your car."

Dawson snorted. He genuinely didn't know how

to be angry with Milo. "And the room number?"

Milo shrugged. "The tag the hotel made you hang on your rear-view mirror has your room number on it."

Dawson shook his head. "You should work for the FBI."

"I don't look good in a suit. Are you going to invite me in?"

With the door held wide, Dawson stepped aside. He automatically inhaled as Milo passed, pulling Milo's sweet scent into his lungs. As he closed the door, Dawson tried not to fall on Milo like a man denied too long. They were hundreds of miles from home. The distance had Dawson forgetting why he couldn't touch Milo.

Milo cast a quick look around before dropping his backpack on the closest table. "Are you on vacation or running away without me?"

Dawson shoved his hands in his pockets and shifted from foot to foot. He didn't know how to respond.

Milo nodded. "So you're running away without me."

"Look, I," Dawson started with no idea where he intended to go with those words.

Milo closed the distance between them, saving

Dawson from trying to gather an explanation. He wrapped his arms around Dawson's waist and held on. His expression, as always, was the sincerest thing Dawson had ever seen. Milo never let him flounder. "I love you."

"Baby, that's—"

"Hush," Milo said, cutting him off. "We swore we wouldn't run away unless we ran together. If you really intend to break every last promise we ever made, then tell me now. Say you're done. Tell me you don't love me anymore. Finally, say you hate me for ruining your life. I want you to end things right now for good... or not."

"You didn't ruin my life."

Milo winced. "We both know I did, so don't stall. You either love me or you don't."

Something about being four hours away from his real life had Dawson throwing in the towel. "The last time we shared a hotel room, your mom called and told me she would drain your bank account, cut you off, and report your car stolen if I didn't find a way to make you go home." Milo's expression snapped closed and the truth kept falling from Dawson's lips. "I had no way to support you and I didn't want you to lose everything you were used to having because of me, so I left. If you stay here now, you'll be stuck at a dead-end job, having coffee thrown in your face too, and I can't be the reason you have to live like that. I need to know you're somewhere painting and making the world beautiful." Dawson's throat swelled and his eyes stung, but he didn't stop. "I love you and I need you to be happy and well cared for, so I'm breaking every promise I ever made to you. This is the end." A tear rolled down Dawson's cheek. He didn't try to stop it. He never, ever wanted to say those words to Milo. Milo finally hadn't left him any other choice.

Tenderness filled Milo's eyes as he swiped the tears from Dawson's cheeks. "For the record, I'm really mad at you right now."

Dawson sniffed. His heart couldn't be any more broken. "I know."

"You should have said something sooner."

Dawson nodded. "I know. You've lost the last three years, hanging on to me when you could've been living your life. I'm sorry for that. I didn't know how to let you go."

Milo pressed his lips to Dawson's, stealing an innocent kiss before pulling away again to meet Dawson's stare. "No. You should've said something sooner, because I cut myself off from Mom three years ago. When I left to meet you that night, my car was already packed, and I didn't go back."

"What?"

Milo nodded. "I had already planned to disappear with you, and I didn't want to go home with my tail between my legs, especially since I never forgave Mom for what she did to you. So I didn't go home. I got a small place above an art studio and started giving lessons two nights a week. Mom never drained my account or reported my car stolen, but we don't really speak anymore."

Dawson floundered. He didn't know what to say or think. Nothing made sense. "But you've been giving me money."

A line appeared between Milo's eyebrows. "Yeah. Every time I sold a painting in your image, I gave you half the money. I told you that." His expression cleared. "Wait. Did you think I've been lying about where the money came from?"

Dawson knew shaky ground when he stood on it. He shook his head. "It's not that. I just didn't argue about taking the money because I thought you didn't need it. If I had known you were having to support yourself on your paintings, I never would've accepted anything from you."

"Baby," Milo said with a breathless-sounding

chuckle. "I have a shit ton of paintings going for tens of thousands of dollars apiece out of an erotic gallery. Did you really think I've been sitting around my mom's place all day every day, doing nothing for the past three years?"

"I hoped you were, yes." Dawson didn't lie or hold back. "Thinking that you were able to do nothing but paint and create is the only thing that's kept me sane while having people yell at me and throw coffee on me for the past three years."

The corners of Milo's mouth lifted in a sad smile. "If it makes you feel any better, I have been doing nothing but painting and creating for the last three years. I've spent countless nights painting until my fingers bled, while hoping gallery showings went well, and just praying you would forgive me one day and let me take care of you."

The pains in Dawson's chest didn't fade. "You're always the one taking care of me. For once, it would be nice if I didn't fail you."

Tears welled in Milo's eyes, breaking Dawson's heart. "Then tell me you don't hate me. That I'm not a mistake. Take it back."

Goddamn. Dawson's knees nearly gave out. He realized in that moment how weak he had always been. If—at any time in the past—Milo had looked at him the way he did now, and asked to be told he wasn't bad, Dawson would have broken. He could not let Milo feel this way.

A growl escaped Dawson as a dam inside him gave way. "Fuck that." He bent and tossed Milo over his shoulder. "You're the best thing that's ever happened to me. Not only are you my best friend, I couldn't hate you even if I saw you murder someone." He tossed Milo onto the bed. "You're my first and only love. That'll never change." He took off Milo's shoes and tossed them aside. "During all the time I've been working at The Back Porch, I've seen countless sexy men come and go. I've still never seen anyone who holds a candle to you." Milo drew a ragged-sounding breath as Dawson peeled off his shirt. After tossing his shirt aside, Dawson unbuttoned his jeans while Milo stared at him with a level of hunger only Milo could. Dawson stopped at unbuttoning his jeans. "I have to leave my pants on. I don't have a condom with me and you're too much of a temptation."

Milo's expression snapped closed. "The last time I checked, neither of us had ever been with anyone but each other, and we've never used a condom." He sat up—like he planned to leave. "If that was your way of telling me you've been with someone else, you can go fuck yourself."

Dawson gently pushed Milo back down and then straddled his body for good measure. "I haven't been with anyone else. You've been leaving the coffee shop with Roscoe and Remington, so I just thought..."

Milo's anger didn't fade. "You thought I would cheat on you," Milo finished for Dawson, making things sound worse.

Dawson took a breath. He wanted to say they hadn't been a couple in years, and it wouldn't have been cheating. The thing was, though, it had felt like cheating every time Dawson had watched Milo leave with a couple who were known for seducing everyone. Not to mention, Dawson had never dated anyone else because he loved Milo. Several times over the years, he had given in to temptation with Milo, with the understanding it was only for the night. But Dawson had never gone elsewhere, because he had always known the truth. He belonged to Milo.

"No. I didn't think you would cheat. I was just hurting myself with the thought of you with them, punishing myself for leaving you in the first place."

Milo shook his head. A smile exploded across his

face. "I've never met anyone else like you. You're good—like to your core. No matter how much it forces you to expose your heart, you always tell the complete truth. How could I ever want anyone else?"

Dawson shrugged. "Easy. I have nothing to offer. Remington and Roscoe are porn kings. They can take care of you."

Milo rolled his eyes. "They're my friends and I paint them together for the gallery. That's it. I don't need anyone to take care of me." Milo lured Dawson closer, tempting him in for a kiss. "All I need is you," Milo whispered as he lifted to meet Dawson and claim his lips. As always, Milo's kiss sucker-punched Dawson. Each and every time their lips met, love washed over Dawson with enough power to steal his breath. He didn't know if other people felt this way in their relationships. All Dawson knew was no one else had ever made him feel this way. Milo wasn't the first person Dawson had ever kissed, but he would be the last. There had never been a single act that happened between them for lust's sake. Everything they did was powered by love. They loved each other. Even when everything stood between them, nothing did.

Dawson tugged at Milo's clothes, needing to feel his bare skin. Even once they were completely nude,

Dawson didn't feel close enough. Still, he didn't move fast. He had learned long ago to savor his moments with Milo. He never knew when it would be the last.

Dawson kissed a path down Milo's chest and tongued Milo's nipple rings. His hand slid lower until he cupped Milo's erection and his fingers curled underneath Milo's balls to play with his guiche piercing. His wicked baby. Always so daring and sexual. Milo squirmed and moaned beneath Dawson's touch. He had so many piercings done for pleasure's sake. The guiche was his favorite for torturing Milo. He moved higher, gripping Milo's cock. He stroked, making sure he didn't miss the magic cross piercing at his crown. That piercing was for Dawson, and goddamn, Dawson couldn't describe the pleasure. Not tonight, though.

Tonight, Dawson wanted to be inside Milo. He wanted to slowly thrust while watching Milo's every expression. He loved the way Milo always bit his bottom lip, trying to hold back his cries. Fuck. Dawson couldn't wait. He quickly rolled from the bed and grabbed the lube from his toiletries bag. With his gaze locked on a panting and waiting Milo, Dawson coated his dick and fucked his palm. Milo made him so goddamn hot. It was the way Milo looked at him—like Dawson owned the only key to his orgasm. Only Dawson could make him fly. No one understood how powerful Milo made him feel. When it came to Milo, Dawson was dark and possessive. He obsessed about him constantly. Dawson would kill for Milo. Die for him.

With his dark thoughts crowding his head, Dawson grabbed Milo's ankle and pulled, hauling him to the edge of the bed. Milo stared up at him with flushed cheeks and his heart in his eyes. Dawson spread Milo's thighs wide and ran his hands down Milo's body, purposely avoiding Milo's cock. The longer he stood there, the more his thunderous thoughts churned, turning darker by the second. Sometimes, he didn't even recognize himself when he was with Milo. Milo belonged to him. He could do anything.

"You look like you can't decide if you want to fuck me or hurt me."

Dawson softened. He unclenched his jaw and forced the tension from his shoulders. "I'm sorry. You know how I get."

Milo nodded. "Don't hide. I love you. Everything about you." Milo's expression turned sultry. He stroked himself as his gaze slid down Dawson's body. "It's been a while. I know what you want." He arched his back, teasing Dawson's inner dark side to come out and play. "Maybe this body has forgotten who owns it. You have been neglecting it, after all. Maybe I've been touching myself beneath the covers while thinking of someone else."

The final word barely left Milo's lips before Dawson snapped. In one quick motion, he flipped Milo onto his stomach. Without thought, he slapped Milo's ass so hard, the sound lingered in the air for a second before reverberating from the walls. Milo scratched at the sheets and moaned. It was too late. Milo had cracked open this side of him.

"What's his name? I'll kill him."

"Oh, god," Milo whimpered as he moved against the mattress, as if needing release.

Dawson spanked Milo again. "Not even God gets to have his name on your lips right now."

"Prove it."

The taunt broke Dawson's brain. He grabbed Milo's hips, hauled him backward, and impaled him. Dawson wasn't gentle. The lovemaking he had pictured earlier was gone.

"Dawson. Fuck. Yes. Holy shit."

Milo's asshole convulsed, sucking him deeper as Milo blew immediately. Dawson wasn't satisfied. He knew Milo had been teasing him about thinking of another man, but Dawson had to ensure Milo never did. It had been one thing for Dawson to torture himself with worry over thoughts of Milo sleeping with Roscoe and Remington. It was a whole other for Milo to fantasize about someone else. Milo's beautiful and perverted mind belonged to Dawson. A sexual act with someone else would wound Dawson. The act wasn't the crime when it came to Milo. It's was Milo's heart, mind, and soul that Dawson wanted. Everything that made Milo irresistible to Dawson were things that couldn't be physically touched. Dawson needed to own those pieces of Milo. Those were things no one else could steal. Dawson could not have Milo picturing anyone else as he came.

"Take it back." The words ripped from his throat on a growl as Dawson slammed inside Milo over and over again.

"You know it's only you," Milo gasped.

Dawson dug his fingers into Milo's skin as he thrust harder, trying to get as deep as possible. "That's not good enough. What's only me?"

Milo white-knuckled the bed and writhed. He whimpered, sounding ready to come again. "Everything is only you. This body. That hole. My heart and every thought. Every orgasm carries your name. I'm yours."

Dawson's shoulders relaxed for real this time. He pulled out and turned Milo in his arms and settled between his thighs. Sweat had Milo's hair sticking to his face. He open mouth sucked air, trying to catch his breath. Dawson pushed the hair out of Milo's eyes and stared down at him. His heart purred—like a tamed lion.

"Goddamn. You're beautiful." Dawson kissed Milo while pushing his way back inside him. He rocked, gently making love to Milo. Dawson tried to make up for his rough treatment. "My sexy, sweet angel," Dawson whispered as he changed angles. He reached between them and stroked Milo's cock. "Sometimes, I jack off on that pink teddy bear you gave me years ago. He's been washed so many times, he's falling apart, but he's all I have of you. You should run from me." Dawson sucked in a sharp breath as he almost came. He was so goddamn close. "Why don't you run from me? You know I'm crazy. You know I might do anything to make sure you're always mine." He squeezed Milo's dick hard, driving his point home.

Milo jerked. Hot cum filled the space between

them. "Because you're mine," Milo whispered as he shook in Dawson's arms.

Dawson's cock twitched hard as orgasm struck. He thrust deep, trying to make the pleasure last as long as possible. With his eyes squeezed shut, Dawson rode out each wave. When his eyes opened, a silver gaze stared up at him, looking every bit as infatuated as Dawson felt. Dawson couldn't look away. Maybe they were both insane. It was possible anyone else would have put a restraining order on either of them by now. Dawson thought they were perfect.

He lowered his head and brushed his lips across Milo's. "I can't believe you put a GPS tracker on my car. Goddamn. That's sexy."

Milo's body shook with laughter beneath him. He swiped his hands through Dawson's hair and held Dawson's face away from his so he could hold Dawson's stare. "I'll slash your goddamn tires if you ever try to leave me again."

Dawson's dick stirred. "Fuck." Even Dawson heard the lust in his curse. "If you keep talking like that, you're going to make me come again."

With an evil-sounding chuckle, Milo dragged Dawson down and nipped at his bottom lip. "Just wait until I tell you the story about the camera I had hidden in that teddy bear before you washed it and ruined it."

A burst of laughter exploded from Dawson. He was so ridiculously in love with this insanity. Dawson never wanted anything else. God help him. Milo could burn down his apartment if he needed to. Dawson didn't see an ounce of instability in that. The only true crazy act he could think of was living without Milo. This love was beautiful to him.

THREE

DAWSON GRABBED his arm before he could escape. In an instant, Milo found himself shoved against the closed door with a pissed-off looking Dawson hovering over him. "What the fuck was that?"

Damn. Milo had almost managed to get away with stealing a kiss. "A kiss," Milo answered, sounding small, even to his ears. He recognized too late how reckless his actions had been, pressing his lips against Dawson's while teaching him how to meditate. He had always been too impulsive.

A deep line appeared between Dawson's eyebrows. "That wasn't a kiss. This is." Without warning, Dawson grabbed Milo's jaw, tilted his head *back, and dove in. His tongue dominated Milo's, stroking and seeking. Milo lost complete control of his hands. They massaged every place they could reach with no permission from Milo's brain. He had never been kissed like this before. Milo never wanted it to end. He was completely swept away. It was no wonder Dawson had girls blowing up his phone all hours of the day. Milo might start stalking him too. With only one kiss, he was completely obsessed.*

MILO COULDN'T STOP STARING at Dawson's mouth. Dawson had always been beautiful. Honestly, Milo didn't think he could be blamed for feeling too much. As a kid, Milo had gone from being terrified of Dawson's large size to fascinated as Milo grew. He wanted to dig his way beneath Dawson's skin and stay. Milo had always felt an overwhelming need for Dawson to feel the same. Sometimes, Milo scared himself a little when it came to Dawson. Actually, he fucking terrified himself. Milo would do anything to stay with Dawson. No matter the cost. This was deeper than love. It was obsession. To his core, Milo knew there was no low too low. Dawson was his.

"You're staring at me."

A smile snapped to Milo's lips. "How would you know? You're supposed to be sleeping."

Dawson stretched like a cat, scooped Milo into his arms, and pulled Milo closer without ever opening his eyes. "I always know when you're staring. It's like I can feel you caressing me with your intensity. And I'm not sleeping because you're not sleeping."

"Does my intensity bother you?"

One eye opened and stared at Milo. "You know it doesn't, but you need your rest."

"I'm too happy to sleep... and too scared."

Both of Dawson's eyes opened at Milo's confession. "Why are you scared?"

Milo shrugged. "You left me the last time we were in a hotel room together. It was the worst moment of my life. I'm not surprised I ended up with a bit of PTSD over it."

"What can I do to help?"

Milo shrugged again, feeling like a kid. "Nothing, I guess. You'll just have to let me watch you while you sleep. Maybe tomorrow night will be different."

Dawson trailed his fingers down Milo's back, looking thoughtful. His eyes were unfocused as if he had turned inside himself. When his gaze latched on to Milo again, Milo knew Dawson's mind was set. "Or we could get up, leave now, and drive the final twenty minutes to Vegas. We could be married by the end of the night. Then you'll never have to feel this way again."

Without a word, Milo rolled away and stood. He found his clothes and started dressing. Dawson didn't budge.

Milo shot him an irritated look. "Are we going, or what?"

Moving much slower than Milo liked, Dawson slipped from the bed. He crossed the room and tugged Milo into his arms. "Hold on for just one second. I want you to be sure."

Milo cupped his face, ensuring Dawson saw the truth in his eyes. "We should have done this that night. When I met you at that hotel, we should've left that second and gotten married. All this pain could've been avoided. This is the only life I want." He kissed the tip of Dawson's nose. "Get dressed." Milo didn't draw an easy breath until Dawson moved to gather his things. Each and every time Milo had gotten close to having the only thing he cared about, something always tore Dawson away from him. Not this time. Dawson belonged to him. No more misunderstandings or meddling mom. Milo was done playing. Tonight, everything would change, even if he had to kidnap Dawson to have his way. Once they were married, nothing would tear them apart again. Milo knew that all the way to his soul.

"I'M GOING to take you away some day."

Dawson tried not to think too much about the warm body on top of him. He kissed Milo's hair, trying to distract himself. "To where?"

"Anywhere. Where would you like to go?" Milo sounded excited—like he had eaten too much sugar or rode the high of life.

"Santa Barbara," Dawson said impulsively, playing along.

Milo's body shook with laughter. "That's random. Why Santa Barbara?"

Dawson massaged Milo's scalp, loving the way his hair felt between his fingers. "That's where I was born. It's where my mom and dad are buried."

Milo shifted positions so he could meet Dawson's stare. "What was your mom like?"

Dawson didn't need to think about it. He remembered every detail. "Beautiful. Soft. She always smelled good. Even though she was too weak to hold me, I would crawl into her lap and hang on. After she died, Dad would tell everyone how much of a shame it was that I was too young to remember her, but nope. I remember everything."

For a long time, Dawson stared up at Milo in silence. There was so much love in Milo's gaze, Dawson knew his mom had chosen Milo for him. There was no way anyone felt this strongly about him on accident. He felt blessed when they were together— like witnessing a miracle.

"That's what we'll do then," Milo whispered, bringing Dawson back on topic. "I'll take you back to her."

Dawson believed. Milo never let him down. The moment Milo turned eighteen, they would run away to Vegas and get married. Then on to Santa Barbara. Milo would make it happen and they would be free. Dawson didn't have a single doubt.

DAWSON COULDN'T BELIEVE they were doing this. They didn't have rings and he couldn't afford them.

As much as Dawson wished that tiny detail didn't bother him, it did. He felt like he had been waiting forever for this moment with Milo and now he couldn't even put a ring on Milo's finger to prove he was taken. Dawson knew he shouldn't feel cheated, but he did. Milo deserved a fairytale wedding, and—as always with Dawson—Milo got a half-ass generic experience that would have sent anyone else running for the hills. Sometimes, he wished Milo would stop settling for him.

The place they chose for their quickie wedding looked like the Valentines' aisle at the drugstore had thrown up inside the building. Dawson tried not to look too closely at anything. Each time a horrible additional detail caught his eye, Dawson winced. He didn't understand how Milo could possibly feel loved or like this day was special in any way.

"I wish I matched what you deserve." The confession burst from Dawson.

Milo cast him a laughing look. "What do I deserve?"

Dawson shrugged. "You weren't at Brett and Roman's wedding, but that. A million-dollar fairytale to match their love."

An ugly-sounding snort escaped Milo. "I'd rather

have a priceless husband and that's what I'm getting."

"Are those your vows?"

Milo held his hand up in the man's face who was attempting to conduct their ceremony while they held a side conversation. "Hold up. I forgot something." He rushed over and picked up his backpack. After digging through it for a minute, he came out with a ring box. "I've been carrying these around since two weeks before I turned eighteen. I thought we would get married right away, but you know." He opened the box and pulled out a set of matching wedding bands. "They probably don't fit anymore, but I want everyone to know I'm yours and you're mine."

"This is the strangest wedding I've ever performed. Was that your vows?"

Dawson knew he smiled like an idiot. He couldn't help it. Even the grouchy wedding conductor they kept ignoring couldn't ruin this. "I do."

Before the guy could say anything more, Milo jumped in. "I do."

The irritated conductor snapped his book closed and blew out a sigh. "By the power invested in me by the state of Nevada, I now pronounce you one soul forever. You may kiss..."

He was too late. Milo had invaded Dawson's space, slipped a ring on his finger, and claimed Dawson's mouth while the guy had still been talking about Nevada. Even as they kissed, Dawson couldn't stop trying to smile. He couldn't believe it. After all this time, and the challenges they had endured, they were married. Even though Dawson knew he would never forgive himself for not telling Milo sooner that Rachel had threatened him, Dawson knew they would be fine. He had married the perfect man, after all. They had suffered enough. Now it was time for some peace and happiness. They had definitely earned it.

"Will you run away with me, sexy?"

Dawson's eyes welled with tears as reality finally caught up with him at Milo's question. "That's always been the plan."

Milo touched his forehead to Dawson's. "Good, because I've been planning this for a long time. There's no going back now."

Dawson felt like he took his first breath of fresh air in years. "Thank god." Even he heard the heartfelt relief in his voice. Dawson had been so tired for so long. He was ready to hand his life over to Milo. Dawson knew he would be safe with him.

———

SINCE MILO HAD FLOWN to get to Dawson, he had to give Dawson directions to get back home. He knew Dawson had to be exhausted, but they would be home soon. By the time they made it, the sun was coming up and they had been awake for a solid twenty-four hours. Milo could have waited until they spent some time sleeping at a hotel in Vegas, but he didn't want to delay this moment another night.

Dawson stared at the large gray stone building with more windows than walls. Milo watched Dawson's every reaction while waiting for him to realize the truth. Dawson leaned forward, eyeing the sign by the door. "Sensual Creations by Milo." As Dawson read the sign aloud, his voice changed, becoming stronger. "Holy shit, Milo. This is your gallery? You have your own gallery in Santa Barbara. What are you doing in L.A. every day?"

Milo tried not to smile like an idiot. "This is more than a gallery. It's also my studio and where I live. I come to L.A. every day to see you. You're worth the drive."

Dawson looked equal parts horrified and impressed as he glanced between Milo and the building. "You make an hour and a half drive every morning to have coffee where I work?"

Milo shrugged. "I love you and I promised I would bring you back to where your mom is buried. So when I had enough money to start my own gallery, I had to make a choice to believe in us." Milo's throat swelled. His voice came out sounding hoarse. "I never stopped believing." His eyes filled with tears and Milo had to take a breath. It got harder to speak by the second. "And I never broke my promise. So, welcome home. We're only about fifteen minutes away from where your parents are buried. I've been taking them flowers about once a month and making sure their graves are well maintained."

Dawson looked away and cleared his throat. With his eyes still locked on the building, Dawson reached over and took Milo's hand. He squeezed before bringing it to his mouth. For a minute, he kept his lips pressed to Milo's hand, as if trying to get his emotions under control. Milo fought the same battle. They understood each other. Always had. Milo didn't doubt for a moment they were soulmates who had found each other from a past life and they would find each other in the next.

"Would you like to see inside?"

Dawson nodded.

Hand in hand, they headed for the building. Milo paused at the front door long enough to show Dawson how to unlock it, using a code that was Dawson's birthday before heading inside. The front door opened into his gallery. Milo turned off the alarm, giving Dawson that code as well.

"This is my gallery. It's open to the public during limited hours and days. Mostly, I sell through word of mouth and galas. Rich people don't like to come in like they're shopping in a store, so they usually set appointments to see my collection."

As Milo watched, Dawson turned in a circle, eyeing everything—like he didn't want to miss a detail. "Holy shit, baby. You've got the gallery you've always wanted. This is amazing."

Milo looked at the large open area with a high ceiling and light pouring in, highlighting his hard work. Pride swelled inside him now that he could finally show Dawson all he had accomplished. When he focused on Dawson again, he found Dawson moving from display to display, inspecting each piece. He couldn't hold back the truth.

"It's all because you believed I could."

Dawson turned his way. "No. You made it because you're an artistic genius. Only an idiot wouldn't believe in you."

Then the world was filled with fools, because no one other than Dawson had believed he could make a dime from being an artist. Milo motioned toward a door to his right. "Come on."

Even though Dawson nodded and headed his way, he dragged his feet while staring at the paintings he passed, like he didn't want to stop staring at Milo's work. Milo couldn't stop beaming. Dawson was the only person who made him feel truly talented. It was strange. People could pay ridiculous amounts for his work, and Milo would think they were only being pretentious. They just wanted his work because it was in or a bit scandalous. He didn't truly believe anyone wanted his work because it moved them. Dawson was the only person who made Milo feel like his art was special and amazing. He needed Dawson.

Milo led Dawson into his studio. It was a mess. Easels and drop cloths were everywhere. Various colors splattered every surface on one side of the room while the other half was pristine. A bed, chairs, and a large bathroom filled the clean side of the room. They were all props for models. There was also a closet stuffed with costumes and various items, but Milo didn't show Dawson that tonight. He motioned at the room in general. "My studio." He kept moving, heading through another door.

Dawson still dragged his feet, trying to look at everything. "Wow."

Milo finally managed to lure him into the next section of the building. As Dawson stepped through the door, Milo kept his gaze locked on Dawson's face. "This is our home."

Dawson froze. His head turned from side to side. The open space was perfect to Milo's mind. It was set up like a vast studio apartment, sectioned by groups of furniture and strategically placed folding walls. The kitchen was in one corner. A sectional couch marked the transition to the living room area. A privacy divider that Milo had painted marked the transition to the bedroom where a king-sized bed sat. There were two more doors. One led into the bathroom and the other into a large walk-in closet.

Dawson met Milo's stare. "This is amazing. Truly. It's perfect."

Milo shrugged, feeling exposed. "It's not the house we grew up in, but it's paid for and it's ours."

"I'm blown away. Seriously. I'm speechless.

You've been working on this the whole time and I've just been wallowing. I don't deserve to live here."

"Don't say that to me." Even Milo heard the hurt and anger in his voice. His feet moved without his permission, going toe to toe with Dawson. "You're the only person who deserves to live here. Not only are you the only person who ever believed I could do this, you're the only person I love, and you're mine. I have the paperwork now to prove it."

While Milo lost his shit, Dawson looked like he was trying not to laugh. His lips twitched and his eyes were bright with happiness. "I love you."

The fight drained from Milo, but not the passion behind his argument. The passion never left Milo. "I love you too."

"I don't know about you, but I'm exhausted."

Milo nodded. "It's been a long and emotional twenty-four hours."

Dawson's hands slid across Milo's hips. "It has been, and I have even more emotional stuff ahead of me. I still have to call Valor and tell him I'm moving."

"And you still have to tell Wrecker you're quitting," Milo added, so there would be no misunderstandings later. Dawson was under his care now.

Dawson nodded. "That too. First, that bed is calling us. We need sleep."

A smile tugged at the corners of Milo's mouth. "Yep. Sleep. We should get on that." He started walking backward, luring Dawson to follow him to bed. "I have just what you need."

Mischief flashed in Dawson's eyes. "I know you do. You promised me you would sleep peacefully and without fear at my side once we were married. We're married."

Milo nodded as he kicked out of his shoes. "We are, but you could still wiggle out of it until it's consummated."

Dawson shook his head, looking severe. "We can't have that. That's a bad loophole. It must be closed."

"Agreed," Milo said, undressing as his walking backward turned into Dawson stalking him. Dawson had the dangerous look in his eyes—the way he always did before he attacked. Milo loved being his prey.

Dawson pulled his shirt up and over his head. "I don't know my way around yet. So find the lube. I want to watch while you get that asshole ready for me."

Milo didn't need to be told twice. He scrambled

to obey. He made quick work of stripping before grabbing the lube from the bedside table. While Dawson finished undressing, Milo settled on the bed. He spread his legs and fingered his asshole with lube, playing with his piercing and teasing Dawson. Dawson gaze never wavered. Milo's cock begged for attention. The bottom half of his body felt heavy with need.

Dawson stroked his erection while he stood beside the bed, watching. "That's it. Stretch yourself."

Milo wouldn't make it long. He never did. Dawson was too hot and sexual. To Milo's surprise, Dawson didn't pounce. He crawled onto the bed and gathered Milo in his arms. With the gentlest of urgings, he rolled Milo onto his side, facing away from Dawson like they were spooning. He stole Milo's kisses as he massaged Milo's hip. Dawson took his time, swiping his cock up and down Milo's crack, teasing him. Finally, Dawson's blunt crown pushed against Milo's asshole. Milo gasped as he shoved his way inside. He felt every inch as it crawled inside him. His greedy body sucked Dawson deeper.

Dawson kissed, licked, sucked, and bit every place he could reach. "Sweet, Milo." His voice was a harsh whisper against Milo's skin. "Your ass feels like it's starving. Hungry for me. I can't believe you married me." His breathless and horny tone never wavered even as he leapt topics into a fresh territory. "I want to tell you you're a fool. Why would you tie yourself to someone like me?"

Before Milo could pull two thoughts together to answer, Dawson grabbed Milo's dick and tugged. His thoughts scattered.

"You know I'm crazy," Dawson said, keeping up the rhetoric. "You know that I'm obsessed with you to the point of being dangerous. Why would you tie yourself to me for life? You know I won't let you get away from me now."

Milo reached over his head and snagged Dawson's hair. He held tight as he tried to ride Dawson's dick and palm at the same time. Dawson's words only fed his lust. "Give me all the crazy. I want it. This is deeper than obsession and you know it. You think you're dangerous." Milo pushed hard against Dawson, trying to take him deeper. "I would fucking kill someone if they tried to take you from me. You are mine."

Dawson rolled, taking Milo with him, and pinning him face down on the bed. Milo gripped the sheet and held on as Dawson slammed inside him. He pounded Milo's ass while Milo writhed in the ecstasy. Pressure climbed his shaft. His mind swirled with lust and love. Dawson was finally his husband. They were married. There was no going back. Never again would they hide. A loud cry ripped from Milo's throat as an orgasm struck. A spasm rocked him while Dawson bit his shoulder and stifled his cries against Milo's skin. The life bled from Milo. His limbs went heavy with exhaustion. They were one now. Right where they belonged.

FOUR

WITH HIS EYES SQUEEZED SHUT, Milo *traced Dawson's lips for so long, he nearly had them memorized. He let himself feel everything. The way each breath caressed his fingers and the way the air changed as Dawson moved closer to orgasm. Goddamn, it was sexy. Even the way Dawson gasped for air felt amazing against Milo's fingertips.*

Dawson's lips changed as he pressed a kiss to the tips of Milo's fingers. "What are you doing?"

Milo didn't open his eyes. He wanted to remember how Dawson's lips felt with that kiss and the words he spoke. "I'm memorizing the shape of your lips. I don't want to forget them, in case this is the last time you touch me." Milo was so tuned in to Dawson's every reaction, he swore he felt the sadness wash over Dawson by nothing more than the feel of his lips.

"Get out your sketchbook. If it'll give you something more than a memory to cling to, you can draw me however you'd like—like you used to do. No one can take that from you."

Milo's eyelids slowly lifted as hope filled his chest. Dawson hadn't let Milo draw him in a long time. "You should let me do paintings of you. I'd hide your face so you wouldn't have to worry about anyone recognizing you. If any of them sell, I'll give you half the profits."

Dawson caressed Milo's cheek. He still looked like he loved Milo. That was what Milo always clung to so he would keep getting up every day. Dawson's thumb traced Milo's bottom lip. When he spoke, Dawson's voice came out sounding hoarse. "Who could turn down that offer? You'll make me a millionaire."

SUNLIGHT FILTERED through the front window, stretching across the hardwood floor. Milo walked along the edge of its reflection, finding the spot where his shadow took up the most space and blocked out the most light. There was a new poem stirring inside him. He played with the words in his head the same way he toyed with the sunlight, rearranging it to suit his mood.

Valor had made the nearly two-hour drive to have lunch with Dawson. Since Milo had a buyer scheduled to look at a gallery piece, he couldn't go with them. As much as Milo wished he could spend every minute with Dawson, he still needed moments like these. Milo had always cherished silence. His creativity thrived when everything went quiet. In two weeks, he was scheduled to do another poetry night at the library. He wanted to have fresh material, something that mirrored the changes his life had undergone since he married Dawson a month ago. His poems always reflected his mood. Dawson deserved to have sonnets and paintings and songs. Milo stretched his arms wide, blocking out even more of the sun's reflection. Dawson deserved the light. Milo dropped his arms and took a step back. A smile touched his lips. He knew what he would say.

The gallery door opened, and the air shifted. Milo turned to greet his new arrival. A young guy with brown hair that brushed the collar of his shirt and needed to be combed strolled through the door.

His dark blue gaze landed on Milo. A smile curved his full lips. He was heart-stopping.

"You must be Milo."

"I am." Even to his ears, Milo sounded distracted. He couldn't stop staring.

The guy's smile turned wicked. "I knew it. You look like an artist."

Milo dropped his gaze to make sure he wasn't covered in paint, which happened more often than not. He was clean. "How do you mean?"

"You look like a dream." He leaned closer. "And that voice, wow. It's amazing. I want to close my eyes and listen to you talk."

Something about the compliments had Milo fighting the urge to narrow his eyes. The guy tossed flattery around too easily for Milo's taste. He wanted to say he couldn't take credit for his voice, since he had been born with it. Unfortunately, the feeling they had met before kept washing over him. He knew this guy, but Milo couldn't place him. "Why do you look familiar to me?"

The too-smooth man rubbed the back of his neck and cast an uncomfortable-looking glance around the room before focusing on Milo again. "Um, I'm Reid King."

Milo's forehead furrowed. "Why does the name ring a bell?"

Reid laughed. It was a deep sound. "I costarred in a film with your mom once."

Milo wracked his brain, since that didn't really narrow things down. It finally hit him. "Oh. You played her son in that one Christmas movie years ago."

A bright smile lit Reid's face. "That's the one."

"I hope you didn't come here hoping to see Mom. We fucking hate each other and haven't spoken in years."

Reid pulled a face Milo couldn't read. "Yeah... no. Truth be told, I didn't much care for your mom when we worked together. I always refer to her as 'the witch' whenever I speak about her to anyone." Reid winced. "I haven't actually used her name in years."

Milo snorted.

Reid didn't give him time to commiserate. "Actually, I have an appointment. I saw one of your paintings at a friend's house recently and she directed me here. We spoke on the phone yesterday."

"Oh." Milo tried to be the professional. "I'm sorry. Recognizing you threw me off my game. So you said on the phone you're in the market for some new art."

"I am..." Reid's gaze slid past Milo a half second before he stepped around him. He headed toward Milo's latest painting of Dawson. "Wow." He moved in close and inspected the image.

Milo stood behind him and did the same. Truthfully, Milo didn't want to sell this one. It was the first image of Dawson since they had married. The second night after their wedding, Milo had straddled Dawson's hips in bed. He had sketched Dawson while Dawson had stroked Milo's cock. Milo had to take a steadying breath while looking at the painting he had rendered in that image. In every painting of Dawson, Milo had done various things to obscure his face, leaving only his mouth and body in focus. This was the only painting in which Dawson smiled. It was a wicked and teasing grin that made Milo's heart beat too fast.

"The symbolism in this one is fantastic. His smile and erection belie the words on his chest. This was a mistake. Amazing."

Milo didn't bother correcting him about the tattoo. Art was subjective, after all. Instead, he stuck with the business side of things. "Each painting is one of a kind. I never create duplicates. So you don't have to worry you'll visit a friend and find your piece isn't as unique as you thought."

Reid glanced over his shoulder. "I'll take it."

Milo bit back a smile. "Just like that. You don't even want to look around or know how much it costs?"

"Money is no object," Reid said, sounding absent. "I'm truly blown away."

Dawson chose that moment to return from his lunch date with Valor. Milo winked but didn't rush to greet him, since he had a customer. When he looked Reid's way again, Reid's gaze moved between the painting and Dawson and back again. Milo jumped in, hoping to shut down Reid's oncoming revelation.

"It's fifteen thousand."

Unfortunately, Reid's gaze never wavered from Dawson. "You're undervaluing yourself." Reid's voice sounded absent. He finally focused on Milo again. "I'm sorry. Is this your model?" he asked, motioning Dawson's way.

For a moment, Milo was torn between being honest and protecting Dawson. Before Milo could decide what to say, Dawson and Valor joined them.

Valor jumped in, saving Milo. "Excuse me. I'm sorry. I hope I'm not ruining a sale for Milo, but I just had to say hello. Your portrayal of Jimmy Cortez was amazing. I saw that play four times during its run at the Coastal Arts Theater."

A bright smile lit Reid's face. He shook Valor's hand. "Thank you. That truly brightens my day. Most people recognize me from cinema, but my heart really lies with live performance. It's refreshing to meet someone with such amazing taste. What's your name?"

"Valor."

Reid's gaze slid Dawson's way again, as if he couldn't help himself. He visibly fought a battle between staying on topic and staring at Dawson.

Milo fought a wave of jealousy. He couldn't risk his reputation by having a fit. This studio was the only way he could ensure Dawson never had to wait tables again.

Reid cleared his throat and tore his gaze away from Dawson once more. "There's no chance of you hurting this sale. I'm sold. He motioned toward the piece behind him. "This one is going home with me."

Valor made a point of not looking at it. "Good choice."

"You're the model, right?" Reid pivoted, obviously seeing his moment and pouncing.

Dawson blushed. It was adorable and distracted

Milo from his jealousy. "Yeah. Usually, people don't know that."

Reid made a dismissive motion. "Don't be embarrassed. You're obviously a huge inspiration to Milo's work." He gestured toward the art surrounding them. "I can't imagine being so powerful that I sparked this much beauty."

Even though every word Reid spoke was true, Milo wished he had been the one who said them. Over the years, Milo had written countless poems trying to express the fire Dawson kept ablaze inside him. In a matter of seconds, on their first meeting, Reid said what Milo should have. It was disheartening. He felt like a failure.

Dawson kept visibly fighting a blush. "Judging by Valor's excitement, you already have a lot to be proud of. I'm just Milo's husband. He already had all the talent before I came along. If he never met me, he would still be the absolute best in his field."

Milo was torn. On one hand, he wanted to bask in Dawson's praise. Milo could feel Dawson's pride when he spoke about Milo's talent. On the other hand, Milo wanted to cry. He fucking hated that Dawson thought he was nothing more than Milo's husband—like he just existed. Before this moment, he hadn't realized how small he made Dawson feel.

It was a gut punch to hear it in front of a guy who was obviously interested in Milo's husband.

Reid's expression turned intense. He sent a subtle and heated glance down Dawson's body. "Like your husband—who plans to charge next to nothing for your image—you undervalue your worth." He visibly tore his hungry stare away from Dawson and focused on Valor. Like a switch was thrown, Reid became bright and cheery as he linked his arm through Valor's. "You should show me around the gallery while Milo wraps up the details of my purchase." They walked away, chatting happily.

For a minute, Milo stared at where they had been while turned inside himself. Before this moment, he hadn't realized how horrible of a job he had done at loving Dawson. Dawson gave him everything and made him feel special. All Milo did was paint him.

Dawson touched his jaw, bringing Milo's gaze his way. "Where's my hello kiss? I missed my wicked angel."

Milo shook off his black mood at Dawson's smile. Dawson didn't look unhappy. "Sorry. I was trying to keep that guy's focus away from you so you wouldn't be embarrassed." He kissed the corner of Dawson's mouth and lingered. His heart automatically beat faster at the contact. No matter how many years passed, Milo's reaction to Dawson never dampened. As Dawson's grip tightened on Milo and their kiss deepened, Milo swore he would try harder to make Dawson feel special. Reid was only the first to recognize Dawson as Milo's model. Once they started going to galas together, everyone would soon realize Dawson was Milo's muse. Milo couldn't keep Dawson to himself forever. He could make him feel like the goddamn treasure he was, though. Milo wouldn't fail him again.

There was something off with Milo today. Dawson couldn't place it. Even though he kept tossing smiles Dawson's way, there was a bitter edge to him. Dawson wanted to be alone and dig for info, but he had to let Milo work. Milo living his true calling was more important than Dawson's sixth sense. Especially since it was entirely possible that Dawson still lived with some insecurities. While there was no way Milo would escape him now, Dawson still knew how it felt to live without Milo. He never wanted to repeat that life.

"It turns out Reid and I both live in L.A.," Valor said, escorting Reid to the counter.

Reid pulled out a black card and passed it Milo's way. Dawson watched Milo while Milo finished Reid's transaction. He murmured something to acknowledge Valor's words, even though he wasn't sure what he said.

Milo handed back the card. "How would you like to handle the delivery? Will you be sending someone, or do you need me to recommend a company that deals in artwork delivery?"

"We're headed in the same direction and I'm in my truck. I could haul it back to L.A. for you."

A smile snapped to Milo's lips at Valor's suggestion. Dawson couldn't look away. "You're just going to toss a fifteen-thousand-dollar painting in the back of your truck?"

The look of horror that crossed Valor's features was priceless. His gaze latched on to Dawson. "People are paying fifteen grand for pictures of you?"

"No," Dawson said, dragging out the word. "People are paying fifteen grand for Milo's talent. No one cares about me."

"I paid fifteen grand for you."

"You should let Milo paint you, Valor," Dawson said over the top of Reid's quietly spoken confession, hoping Milo didn't hear. "He's amazingly talented and any canvas he touches turns to gold. It would be a brilliant way for you to make some extra money."

Valor waved off his suggestion. "No one in their right mind would buy a painting of me."

"I would."

Everyone fell silent at Reid's words.

The moment he had everyone's attention, Reid ran with it. "We should set that up. What do you say, Milo? Do you do private commissions?"

"Not for less than thirty thousand."

Dawson fought his eyebrows as they tried crawling to his hairline. Milo looked serious, leaving no doubt to Dawson's mind that he had heard Reid's earlier comment about paying for Dawson's picture to own Dawson's image and not Milo's talent.

Reid didn't back down. "Sold."

They both focused on Valor, but Reid was the one who did the cajoling. "What do you say? If you can come to terms with Milo on a fee, would you like to be nailed against my wall?"

Dawson bit his bottom lip, trying not to laugh.

Valor's open discomfort fled at Reid's suggestive tone. "I'm in."

Milo, Reid, and Valor fell into a discussion about what they needed to do to get the most out of their painting. While they made plans and Reid gave Milo half the money up front, Dawson watched the way the light played across Milo's features. His silver eyes looked almost gray today. Dawson felt himself falling even more in love with Milo every second. He was so fucking proud to be Milo's husband. Dawson had never had any actual dreams beyond that. Milo was so massively talented that just loving him was a full-time job. Maybe most people wouldn't be content with that. Dawson was more than happy simply being Milo's other half. He got to know that he had inspired beauty to flow from this amazing man. Not many people could say that. Not many people could claim to have been in the presence of greatness, much less was loved by it. Milo's gaze slid his way. Dawson's heart skipped a beat. His breath left him. The world looked so much brighter than it had two months ago. This was a good life. He would do anything to keep it.

FIVE

FOR THE HUNDREDTH TIME, Dawson tugged at his collar on the sly. He wasn't used to dressing up, but it seemed like he had been doing a lot of it lately. Between everyone he knew getting married and now his first gala, Dawson should have been used to suffocating in his clothes, but he wasn't there yet.

"For fuck's sake. Take off your tie and undo a few buttons."

Dawson fought a smile. He should have known Milo would spot his every move. "No. This is my first time at one of your events. I'm supposed to be the supportive husband. Not the whiny bitch who can't stand nice clothes." Just the idea had Dawson curling a finger around his collar again and tugging.

Milo spun, going toe to toe with him. His eyes

flashed with irritation. "Jesus Christ. This is my gala and you're my husband. We'll do what we want." He snagged Dawson's tie and pulled it loose before going to work on the buttons of his shirt.

Dawson sucked a deep breath as the material parted away from his throat. "Damn. That's good."

Milo froze. His gaze moved from his hands to Dawson's face. "Don't talk like that. You will embarrass me if I'm walking around with a tent pole in my pants."

A bark of laughter burst from Dawson, bringing several eyes their way. Dawson bit his bottom lip, trying to reel himself back in.

Milo's lips turned up in the corners in a knowing smile as he straightened Dawson's shirt. "Happiness looks damn sexy on you, baby."

Before he could respond, Reid appeared at Milo's side. "Everyone is looking this way in anticipation. They can't wait to see if you plan to strip your muse completely bare. I know my breath is held and my hopes are high."

Dawson rolled his eyes.

Milo wasn't as nice. "You're doing a lot of talking for someone whose breath is held."

While Dawson's eyebrows tried climbing to his hairline, Reid didn't seem the least bit offended. In fact, he kept talking like nothing happened. "Congrats on your big night, Milo. People are pulling out their wallets right and left. You'll soon be able to buy Dawson a proper house."

Dawson opened his mouth to say Milo had already done that, but Reid plucked the empty champagne glass from Dawson's hand, jumping topics again.

"You look thirsty. I'll take care of you."

Milo pinched the spot between his eyes.

Dawson immediately forgot about Reid. "Are you okay? Do I need to sneak you out the back?"

Gorgeous silver eyes latched on to Dawson, and Dawson forgot what they were talking about. After a moment, a sweet smile touched Milo's lips and he stroked Dawson's cheek. "You never stop amazing me with the way you don't notice anyone but me."

Dawson felt his forehead furrow. "Why should that surprise you? There is no one else but you."

With a chuckle, Milo shook his head—like he thought Dawson was adorably blind or something. He made a dismissive motion. "What do you think of Reid? I can't believe Valor brought him tonight."

With a shrug, Dawson glanced around, looking for Valor. He had forgotten about Valor until Milo reminded him other people existed. Dawson needed to be a better friend. This wasn't Valor's crowd either. No doubt he was having a terrible time. He spotted Valor speaking closely to Reid's ear and looking right at home. Dawson shook his head. "I know Valor is a bit older than Reid, but I'm sure he will be okay. I don't think he's the type to get hurt. As long as I've known him, he's dated a lot of younger guys. He never seems bothered when they're gone." When Milo didn't respond, Dawson's gaze moved back Milo's way. Milo stared at him like he couldn't believe the words leaving Dawson's lips. "What?"

Milo shook his head. "I love you."

Dawson didn't understand what was going on with Milo tonight. He seemed tense. Dawson chalked it up to nerves with everyone looking at Milo's work and judging him. "I love you too."

A woman dressed in black appeared at Milo's side. "Milo, there are a few people who would like to speak with you. They already have their wallets out and want more."

Dawson gave Milo an encouraging nod. "Get lost. Your fans are waiting. Your biggest one will stay here and out of the way."

Milo took a step back while holding Dawson's stare. He didn't turn away until Dawson winked. They knew each other. Milo needed Dawson to be okay while he worked. That was what Dawson intended to do. He might be out of his comfort zone, but he was surrounded by Milo's work and he was damn proud of his husband. Dawson would stand in the corner all night if Milo needed him to do so.

Reid joined him. "Valor is waiting in the lengthy line for our champagne. We decided one of us should keep you company. Otherwise, Milo might say fuck it and walk away from dozens of potential clients."

That was true. He couldn't let Milo think he was bored. "Thank you. I appreciate it. Obviously, I'm out of my element, but I want Milo to be a hit."

Reid kept his gaze locked on the crowd. He looked like the perfect bored millionaire. "Milo is already a hit. This is just another show to him. I am curious, though. Valor says this is your first event. How is that possible? Milo's images of you span years and you are his husband. Why has he kept you hidden?"

Dawson opened his mouth to say Milo hadn't done any such thing, but that wasn't entirely true. In a lot of ways, Dawson had been a secret, but not by anyone's choice. "It's a long and boring story that doesn't matter any longer."

Reid shrugged. "We likely have a minute. That was truly an unending line at the champagne table."

Dawson flashed Reid a pained smile. "No offense, but it's not really any of your business and I'd rather not relive it."

Reid didn't as much as flinch. "I didn't mean to offend you." He set his hand on Dawson's arm and held his stare, ensuring Dawson saw the guilt in his eyes.

Since Reid looked genuinely apologetic, Dawson chose to let it go. "You didn't." Dawson sighed, throwing everything to the wind. "It's his mom. She's a wretched bitch and did everything she could to keep us apart. Like I said, it's a long story. She caused a lot of hurt and bitterness, but she didn't break us. Nothing can break us." Dawson held Reid's stare, hoping his words were heard. He knew Milo and Reid thought he was blind. He wasn't. Dawson knew Reid was constantly flirting. He didn't understand why, since Reid knew he was married, and Reid was supposed to be out with Valor. But Dawson had spent enough time with rich people to know they thought nothing was off limits to them. Dawson was. No one could take him from Milo.

Reid dropped his hand from Dawson's arm. "Do you like it here in Santa Barbara? I have to say it's growing on me."

Dawson accepted the change in topic. "I love it here. This is where I grew up."

A genuine smile touched Reid's lips, transforming him into an actual person. "Seriously? I thought you were an L.A. boy through and through. I grew up in the Midwest."

As Reid fell into a story about growing up in a small town while having big city dreams, Dawson fought the urge to look Milo's way. While Reid was much more likable while not play acting, Dawson still worried over Milo's earlier mood. He didn't want anything ruining Milo's night. That included himself and that was why he had to pretend he was having an amazing time, no matter how bad he wanted to go home.

THE LONGER REID and Dawson stood in the corner with theirs heads together and talking in their own bubble, the darker Milo's mood became. While Milo was trying his damnedest to give Dawson a better life than waiting tables, he couldn't give him the kind of life someone like Reid could. As Reid had pointed out, Milo hadn't bought Dawson a real house. Living in his gallery probably didn't feel like much of a home to Dawson. As much as Milo wanted to rush to Dawson's side and shoo Reid away, he had to sell some paintings tonight if he hoped to give Dawson the life he deserved, eventually.

Milo spent a good three hours not looking Dawson's way at all. It was hell and wrecked his mood, but he couldn't watch Dawson with someone else. Milo simply slipped farther and farther into his depression until they were halfway home.

"Do you want to tell me what's wrong? Everyone loved your paintings."

Milo took a breath and counted to three in his head before answering. "I'm just tired." It wasn't a lie. Milo was fucking exhausted. He had been hanging on to them by his fingernails for years now. Milo couldn't be more tired of having to fight for them.

Dawson linked fingers with him and drove the rest of the way in silence. The moment they were home, Dawson leapt from the car to get to Milo's side. He opened the door, unbuckled Milo's seatbelt, and lifted Milo into his arms. He carried Milo to the house like he would a child. Dawson kept kissing his forehead along the way. By the third time, Milo felt himself melting. It wasn't Dawson's fault that Reid was interested in him. Only a fool wouldn't be. Just because Reid wanted Dawson, that didn't mean Dawson would bite. Milo could feel Dawson's love. This wasn't something easily broken.

Milo let himself relax in Dawson's hold. The horrible night slipped away. Once Milo finished Reid's commissioned piece, they never had to see him again. This would pass. Milo had always been the jealous type and it had never been Dawson's fault. It was just that Dawson had always been sexy and popular. He had been part of the in crowd and Milo had not. Having someone like Reid trying to catch Dawson's attention brought back a lot of old insecurities. At the end of the day, it was Milo that Dawson carried to bed.

Dawson set Milo on the edge of the mattress and gently undressed him. Milo let it happen. His heart couldn't stop eating every second of Dawson's affection alive.

"Why are you perfect?"

Dawson met Milo's stare at the question. "I don't feel perfect. In fact, I feel pretty damn useless."

Milo stroked Dawson's face. "Why would you say something like that?"

With a shrug, Dawson tucked Milo into bed. "You worked so hard tonight, trying to support us, and I didn't know how to help. I tried to stay in the corner and out of the way. You shouldn't have to carry us alone, but I don't know what I can do to make things easier."

"You could hold me." Milo didn't even care if he sounded needy. He was. Milo required snuggles.

Dawson immediately stripped and joined Milo beneath the covers. "That's one area I've definitely got covered." Dawson tugged Milo into his arms and squeezed him against his chest. He kissed the top of Milo's head. "This is the part that almost killed me over the years." Dawson's admission had Milo's throat swelling. He didn't stop there. "When your mom kicked me out, I swear I didn't sleep for a week afterward. I was so used to having this every night and then you were gone. Never again. All these cuddles are mine."

Milo hid his face and smiled against Dawson's chest. He swore the only time he breathed properly was in Dawson's arms.

Dawson kept talking, making Milo's muscles relax. "Hey, I had money saved to move to Nevada. We should take that and go on a honeymoon. I didn't really think about it, because of my move and every day with you is like a vacation, but we should do it. Let's go somewhere far away for a couple of weeks."

Milo's smile grew. "I like this plan. Don't use

your savings, though. We can afford to go anywhere after tonight. Also, I have a poetry reading at the library next week that I don't want to miss. They've been really good to me. But that'll give us time to pick a spot and book everything. Do you have any place in mind?" Dawson was quiet for so long that Milo turned his chin up to see Dawson's expression. A tiny smile hovered on Dawson's lips, fascinating Milo. "What?"

Dawson chuckled. "Do you remember that time we lied about there being a school trip and went camping?"

A loud groan escaped Milo. "I don't want to do that again. By the end of the week, I was a sweaty hot mess. You had to kill a snake that I'm pretty sure was venomous and we both ended up with a horrible rash from poison oak."

Dawson nodded. "I know, but everything else about that week was amazing. It was just us and I got to dream it would only be us forever. We don't have to go camping, but I wouldn't mind something really disconnected from the world like that."

"Glamping?" Milo suggested.

Dawson squeezed Milo tighter. "Yes. I could get behind that. No internet, but also no tents. Just you and me in a camper in the middle of the woods with nothing but time."

Fuck. Milo wanted to leave that second. He couldn't wait to have Dawson all to himself with no interruptions. After all, Dawson was right. That week of camping together had given them a taste of what their future would be, and Milo's determination to be Dawson's husband had grown into an obsession. That being their honeymoon seemed almost serendipitous.

"I can't wait," Milo whispered more for himself than Dawson. Dawson always knew exactly how to fix everything. Tonight was no different. Milo felt the weight of the world disappear. Everything was perfect.

SIX

DAWSON GRABBED *a leather-bound book from Milo's dresser and started flipping through the pages. "What's this?"*

Milo lost his breath. In a panic, he snatched the book away. His heartbeat pounded in his ears. "That's personal."

The wicked light flashing in Dawson's eyes made Milo's mouth go dry. "Ah. Is it your diary?"

Milo swallowed. His palms began to sweat. "No."

Dawson's expression shifted, as if he realized he made Milo uncomfortable. "I'm sorry. You know I would never force you to tell me anything."

Gah. Dawson was so infuriating. Milo knew he could put his journal away right now. Dawson would never ask about it again, but then Milo would always feel like he had hidden something from him. "It's poetry."

To Milo's surprise, Dawson sat forward, looking intrigued. "Really? I didn't know you wrote poems. May I read them?"

Heat crawled up Milo's cheeks. He could not let Dawson read his personal thoughts. All it would take was two pages and Dawson would know exactly how bad Milo had it for him... and for how long. Milo cleared his throat. "I'd rather you didn't."

Dawson sat back. "Oh. Okay. Do you want to watch a movie or something?"

Milo sucked in a breath. Dawson's disappointment was like getting punched in the gut. Milo couldn't explain why he felt such a deep connection to Dawson; why he always felt what Dawson felt. With a deep breath for courage, Milo opened the journal. He flipped through the pages until one poem stood out above the rest. Before he could change his mind, he read the words aloud. "His eyes haunt me. It's that way, I guess. I know this is how things will always be. He'll forever leave me a mess. His lips taste different than I expect. I thought cherries and got respect. He held my hand today where anyone could have seen. I'm the one who pulled away, recognizing how far we've careened.

The second I was alone, I cried. No one understands how much I don't want to hide. Life was an empty void before he let me steal that first kiss. Now I live in constant terror of losing this."

Milo's hands shook as he closed the book. His gaze lifted. Dawson stared at him with such intensity that Milo's first instinct was to run. Instead, he stood still as Dawson came to his feet and closed the distance between them. "I have to taste that talent."

Milo melted as Dawson's lips touched his. The way Dawson made him feel comfortable and proud in his every endeavor was empowering as hell. Every day, Milo fell a little deeper for Dawson while Dawson built him into being fearless in his art. If he ever made a career from the words and images living inside his head, it would be all due to Dawson. He was Milo's backbone.

DAWSON WAS CONSTANTLY BLOWN AWAY by how Milo could step up to a microphone in front of a crowd without batting an eyelash. He looked like he belonged. Milo could bare his heart to a room full of strangers in the most beautiful poetry imaginable without feeling the least bit exposed. He never stopped wowing Dawson. In fact, Dawson fought the urge to sit on the edge of his seat. He couldn't wait to hear what Milo had to say. Dawson already knew it would be amazing.

While Milo got ready to do his reading, Dawson sat in the audience next to Valor, who had become a surprising supporter of everything Milo did. Valor would never know how much Dawson appreciated him. Milo deserved to have a parental figure supporting him. It was the one thing Dawson couldn't give him. Dawson's chest swelled with pride as he watched Milo move around the stage. Milo looked relaxed and in his element. In a long sleeve shirt that molded his body and dark jeans, Milo also looked sexy as fuck. Dawson kept catching himself biting his bottom lip as he stared at his husband. It didn't help that Milo kept tossing him heated glances. In the past six years, Dawson had enjoyed Milo's body countless times and in every way imaginable, but he never tired of him. He wanted more. Dawson couldn't wait to be holed up in a camper for two weeks with Milo. It was already parked in their driveway and just waiting for Milo and Dawson to drive away. Dawson wanted to shut out the world and mark Milo as his. Goddamn, he was in love.

"I guess I'm getting stood up."

At Valor's random comment, Dawson tore his gaze away from Milo to focus on him. After all, Valor had shown up for Milo. Dawson needed to pay attention to their guest. "Oh? Did you have a date tonight?"

Valor nodded. His gaze scanned the room, never meeting Dawson's stare, as if searching for his mystery date. "Reid said he would meet us here tonight. I think I scare him a little."

Dawson fought the urge to roll his eyes. He wanted to say he didn't like Reid and Valor was better off without him, but Dawson kept his opinions to himself. Valor deserved better than some guy who flirted with everyone else. Just because Reid was famous, that didn't make him special. From Dawson's experience, famous people fucking sucked. Instead of saying any of that, he patted Valor's knee. "I'm sorry to hear that. You'll be too much for the wrong people. Only the right guy will be able to handle you once things get intense."

Valor snorted as he finally met Dawson's stare. "Why are you so old on the inside? I'm twice your age. I should be the one giving advice, but you've always been this way. It's like you were born an old man."

With a smile, Dawson looked away. "An old soul. That's what my dad used to say."

The lights dimmed and the stage brightened. Dawson fell silent along with everyone else. He didn't want to miss a second of Milo's performance. Without thinking, he leaned forward, trying to get closer to Milo.

A hand landed on Dawson's shoulder a half second before lips touched his ear. "Come outside with me?"

Dawson's gaze snapped to the man interrupting Milo's show. Reid stared back at him. He looked like hell. His hair was a mess and there were dark circles under his eyes. Dawson didn't give a shit about any of that. It was Milo's night.

Dawson motioned toward the stage. "The reading is starting."

Even though Dawson could practically feel Valor staring daggers over his shoulder in Reid's direction, Reid didn't back down. "It's important. I wouldn't ask if it wasn't an emergency."

Dawson shook his head. He wasn't doing this. There was nothing Reid could say to drag him away from Milo's show. He barely knew this guy, yet Dawson felt certain Reid was up to no good.

Reid motioned toward the door. "You can either hear about it now or on the news later."

Goddamn it. Dawson was exhausted. He pushed to his feet and headed for the door without looking back. Hopefully, he could deal with this fast and get back to his seat before he missed too much. The second they were outside, Dawson spun on Reid, ready to blast him.

Reid spoke fast, stealing the air from Dawson's lungs. "Milo's mom is blackmailing me to ruin your marriage."

"What?" The question sounded like it came from somewhere else as the world narrowed to a pinpoint. They were supposed to be done with Rachel. She was out of their lives. Dawson didn't understand.

Reid licked his lips, looking nervous. His gaze scanned the parking lot, as if he expected they were being watched that moment. "Listen. Rachel has kept tabs on Milo since he moved out. When she found out he married you, she contacted me. I don't know if I'm the only gay man she knows or if I'm just the only one she has dirt on, but she wanted me to seduce Milo away from you. She thought it would be easy. She thought that Milo wanting you was all about a lack of options and he would easily fall for me." Reid kept talking while Dawson fought the urge to kill someone. "She just wanted you out of the picture, but the moment I saw Milo's gallery, I knew he couldn't be seduced. Every image was unmistakably you. I know obsession when I see it and I knew there was no way he could see past you to fall for me. So I chose another path—to undermine him. Drop a few words here and there. Make him question if he's good enough for you. I knew Rachel wouldn't care how I accomplished the task as long as you two ended."

Dawson scrubbed his forehead. He couldn't believe his ears. He thought they were past this. Rachel was supposed to be nothing but an awful memory. "I don't understand. Why would you do this? What kind of person are you?" Dawson's voice grew louder by the second as the full picture came together. Rachel was back to scheming. This guy had been intentionally harming Dawson's marriage and he had been seeing Valor too. Every new thought Dawson had, the uglier the situation became. "Where does Valor come into play in this? Why would you hurt him? What has he done to anyone to deserve this?"

Reid's hands rose, as if to show he had nothing before falling again. "Valor... he just... he wasn't supposed to happen. I wasn't supposed to meet him, but I did. And now, I'm just... I don't fucking know. I like him and he doesn't realize that I'm this really horrible person who's done really terrible things to get where I am. He's the reason I'm telling you all this. Rachel won't hesitate to tell the world everything she knows about me, but I don't want to do this. Valor loves you like a son and I genuinely like Milo and you. You're all nice people. I don't want to do this."

"What in the fuck is going on out here?" Valor said, appearing from nowhere. "You missed Milo's show."

A growl rose in Dawson's throat. He was so sick of life being hard. "Goddamn it. Is he still inside? Is he on his way out here?" Dawson didn't want to tell him this bullshit. He didn't want Milo walking into the middle of this horrible nightmare without warning.

Valor made a helpless gesture while looking angrier than Dawson had ever seen him. "He saw you leave with Reid and he just quickly did his thing and left out the back."

Dawson fought the urge to pull out his hair. "What do you mean he left? Our car is right there," Dawson said, pointing toward their parked car.

"I don't fucking know." Valor sounded every bit as aggravated as Dawson felt. "He said he was out of here, and then he just walked away. So I came looking for you. Someone needs to start talking."

With an angry sweep of his arm, Dawson motioned Reid's way. "Then talk to this one right here. He seems to be the only goddamn person who has any clue what's happening. I have to find Milo. Fucking Rachel and her goddam bullshit. I'm so damn sick of this shit." Dawson cursed and stamped his way to the car, uncaring if he looked like a raving lunatic as he left without saying goodbye. He was angry and scared. Milo had walked away and gone god only knew where. Rachel was still out to destroy them, and Dawson didn't know where to go with that. Everything hurt. He felt the same way he had the night Rachel had threatened to strip everything from Milo if Dawson stayed with him. Dawson felt like he wasn't strong enough or good enough to hold them together while Milo's mother tore them apart. Life wasn't supposed to be this way. Parents weren't supposed to destroy their children. Dawson didn't know how to fight that.

Dawson climbed behind the wheel of his car, feeling more determined than ever. Milo was his husband. They were the only family they needed.

He would find Milo and fix everything. Even if they had to live off the grid and in a tent for the rest of their lives, Dawson would shield Milo from any more pain. Rachel had fucked with them for the last time. Dawson was done.

VALOR HAD ALWAYS ATTRACTED YOUNGER men. In truth, he preferred men his age, but the twenty somethings always found him. Since he had never been interested in anything long term, he hadn't minded the fun. They fucked and went their separate ways. No feelings got hurt. Younger guys were always on the move and he was just a stopping point. It was an arrangement that worked for him. Valor's feelings weren't involved. In fact, there had been times he had wondered if he had a heart. The only reason he knew he could love anyone was because he loved Dawson, but that was a fatherly affection.

As he stared at Reid, wondering what in hell had just run him over, Valor realized he did in fact have feelings to hurt. At first, meeting Reid had been one hell of an ego boost. Reid was famous, sexy as fuck, and Valor had already been a fan. Then they had gone on a few dates. No sex. Proper dates. Talking, getting to know each other, and hours of genuine connection. There had been a spark. Now, fifteen minutes after Dawson went after Milo, Valor couldn't stop staring at this beautiful liar with his heart in his throat.

"What does she have on you?"

Reid shook his head. A sad smile touched his lips. "Enough."

Valor fought to separate his feelings from the situation. It was impossible. He had already harbored some hatred for Rachel for hurting Dawson. Now this. Valor had a lot of anger at the moment and nowhere to go with it. "Enough to ruin your career or enough to send you to prison? There are vastly different levels of enough."

Reid's throat moved as he visibly swallowed. His eyes looked haunted. Guilty. "Enough to ruin my reputation and my career. Enough to keep you looking at me the way you are now."

"How am I looking at you?"

A muscle twitched in Reid's jaw. "The way she does."

Something about Reid's words and his expression had a horrible thought growing in Valor's head. He had been a fan of Reid's long before he met him. Reid hadn't done anything beyond stage work in years. His only major films had been done when he was only a kid. Rachel wasn't a stage actress. That meant, whatever she knew, had to be from when Reid was a child. "I thought you only worked on that one movie with her."

Reid nodded. "It was enough."

Valor felt like his lungs might collapse. "But you were only like twelve back then. Have you stayed friends with her over the years?"

Reid's expression said all Valor needed to know. "That woman is vile."

Valor closed the distance between them. He found himself rubbing Reid's arms, trying to comfort him. "Tell me what she has." He kept his voice soft, trying to keep Reid from bolting.

Reid's throat moved again. He looked like a runner. After a moment, Reid's eyes fell closed—like he couldn't look at Valor while making his confession. "She knows I had to sleep with the director to keep that role with her."

Valor felt sick. Reid had only been twelve. That was rape, and Valor couldn't make his tongue shape the words. He tried to stay calm. "How does she know this? Does she have proof?"

Reid nodded. "Video. Apparently, he recorded the encounter and sold it to her."

Valor tried not to show his rage or his hope. He was so close to having Rachel right where he wanted her, and it hurt his chest for it to happen this way. "Are you sure? Did she show you this video?"

Reid nodded again.

It got harder for Valor to hide his emotions. He wanted to kill someone, but Reid needed him to be calm and in charge. "How did she show you? Did she show you on her laptop?"

Reid shook his head. "She texted me a small clip. Enough to prove she had it."

Valor pulled Reid in for a hug and kissed his forehead. "It's okay. I'll take care of you. You don't have to be scared anymore. Do you trust me?"

Reid clung to Valor's shirt. Valor felt him nod as he dropped his head to Valor's shoulder. Valor's attention split between comforting Reid and plotting Rachel's demise. She wouldn't hurt anyone else he loved. Valor would make sure of that. After years of watching Dawson suffer and not knowing why, Valor finally had that bitch right where he wanted her, and he fully intended to make sure she never hurt anyone else ever again.

DAWSON FELT SICK. Milo had always been capable of doing anything. While Milo had grown up in an enormous house with all the riches anyone could dream to have, he had been completely denied love and human touch until Dawson had given it to him. Milo had been expected to be accomplished and quiet. He was meant to give the illusion of being the perfect son to a mother who cared not at all about his existence beyond how he made her look in the court of public opinion. Dawson had tried his damnedest to be everything Milo needed. A lot of damage had already been done, though. Milo had never much cared if he lived or died. Dawson's love was what kept him grounded. That was why, even when Dawson had been forced to keep his distance, he had ensured Milo had still known he was loved, and Dawson had never really dated anyone else. The knowledge that Milo had seen him leave with Reid and now thought the worst was killing him. Dawson swayed wildly between wanting to search every street for Milo and racing to get home.

The lights were on inside when Dawson pulled into their driveway. He barely had the car in park before he leapt out and raced inside. He wouldn't breathe easy until he set eyes on Milo. The gallery was empty, but the door to the studio stood open and banging sounds came from inside. Dawson hurried that way. He slid to a stop inside the doorway. Wet paint splattered the room and several finished pieces were completely destroyed. Milo walked in a circle, dragging a wide paintbrush with red paint across every single one of his works in progress. Horror overcame Dawson. Milo was intentionally destroying all his hard work.

"What are you doing?"

Milo didn't even look his way as he shrugged and kept painting a thick red line through the middle of his work. "It's all bullshit. None of this will ever give you the life you deserve. It matters not at all."

Dawson moved deeper into the room. "What are you talking about? Stop, Milo. You're ruining everything you've worked so hard to make."

Milo didn't listen. In fact, Dawson wasn't sure Milo was completely there any longer. "Why did you come back? You left with Reid. He can give you a better life than I can."

"Baby, no. I didn't leave with Reid. He asked me to step outside so he could explain why he's been trying to ruin our marriage. I was outside yelling at him when you left me."

Milo froze. His face turned Dawson's way. Dawson almost took a step back. His heart twisted in his chest. Milo looked destroyed. "I'm very tired," Milo whispered, breaking Dawson's heart. "I've been working so hard for you for so long. I don't think it's supposed to be this hard."

Dawson didn't like the way this was headed. Milo sounded like he had given up—like he had finally been pushed too far. He picked up more paint and smeared it across one of the images. "You're supposed to be mine now. I'm not supposed to have to fight anymore." Milo pushed, shoving the easel to the floor and sending paint brushes flying.

Dawson crossed the room. He couldn't let this happen. Milo had mostly remained calm through their years of struggle. Dawson couldn't let him come apart now that they had finally found their place. Before Milo could do any more damage, Dawson snatched him off his feet and held him against his chest. He spoke against Milo's ear, trying to calm him. "Stop it, baby. No one comes between us. From that first stolen kiss, I've always been yours. Tell me how to fix this. I'll do anything."

Milo went limp in his arms. He sniffed and Dawson wanted to be the one who destroyed things.

"Don't cry," Dawson begged. "Do you want me

to drive back to the library and punch Reid in the face? I will. You can watch."

He felt more than saw Milo make a helpless gesture. "I just..."

"I know," Dawson said, stroking Milo. "Me too. We were supposed to have a fresh start here. We weren't supposed to have to fight your mom or public opinion any longer. I thought we would get to finally have the peace we deserve."

Milo went still. Dawson swore he stopped breathing. "What does Mom have to do with this?"

Dawson spun Milo in his arms. He didn't want to tell Milo the truth, but he couldn't avoid it forever. "Your mom blackmailed Reid to come between us. He was supposed to seduce you, but as soon as he saw the gallery and that I was the subject of your paintings, he knew you wouldn't cheat. So he chose to undermine us instead. Flirt with me. Drop hints that you're not good enough. But I guess he liked us better than he expected, and things got complicated."

While Dawson had expected rage, that wasn't what he got. Instead, Milo seemed to deflate even more. "Dawson." His voice sounded so weak and small that tears sprang to Dawson's eyes.

"What is it, baby?"

Milo took a ragged-sounding breath. "I'm really tired."

The tip of Milo's nose was red, and his eyes looked weary. Milo also had paint all over him. Dawson tugged at Milo's clothes. "That's okay, angel. That's why you have me." He worked at undressing him. "I'm going to clean you up, and then you're going to go to bed in the camper while I drive. When you wake up, we'll be somewhere new."

"Are we running away?"

Dawson shook his head. "We are going on our honeymoon—like we have earned the right to do. You're mine, I'm yours, and it's long past the time everyone just fucking accepted that. There is nothing shameful or ugly about us. We are beautiful and meant to be. Hell, we are fucking blessed. Do you know how many people never find their soulmate and we met as kids? We got to grow up together and know each other in ways other people never experience." Dawson finished stripping Milo while keeping up his rant. "I'm not ashamed of how we fell in love. My only regret is that I let your mom make me believe that anything was bigger than the two of us together." Dawson pulled off his shirt and tapped his chest at his tattoo. "That doubt was the mistake. Not trusting us to overcome everything thrown at us, that was the biggest mistake of my life. It's one I won't make again. So, if you're tired of fighting, it's okay. I'll take over, because that's who we are. We're a team."

Milo blinked. A tear rolled down his cheek. "I love you." It was a harsh whisper that tore at Dawson's heart, but he knew the words came from Milo's soul.

"I love you too."

They would be fine. Hell, they would be perfect. Even if Dawson had to drive Milo to the middle of nowhere and live off the land, they would never be apart again. Dawson would see Rachel dead before he let her ruin them.

———————

As DAWSON FIRED the shower to life and checked the temperature, Milo watched him in silence. He worried he might have gotten a little crazy tonight. Not once, in all their years together, had Dawson made Milo feel unstable. Milo knew he was, though. He probably needed to work on that. Milo hadn't meant to overreact. Truthfully, he wasn't even completely sure what happened. One second, he had been burning alive beneath Dawson's heated stare.

The next, Dawson had been leaving Milo's poetry reading with another man and Milo had snapped. One cab ride later, Milo watched himself destroying his studio like he witnessed it through someone else's eyes.

He shouldn't have been surprised his mom still worked behind the scenes to control him. The thing was, Milo was just too damn tired to care about anything. Dawson still loved him. That was all that mattered. He would not give his mom the attention she sought by hunting her down and lashing out at her. As long as Dawson still loved him, then everything else could get fucked.

Dawson stripped, pulling Milo's focus away from the disastrous night. Unfortunately, the moment he stopped thinking about everything leading up to this moment, the shaking set in. His teeth chattered. Reality came crashing down. He had destroyed close to two hundred thousand dollars' worth of work. His mom had sent someone into their lives to break up their marriage. Between his mom and his own craziness, Milo would never escape the constant drama. Milo wrapped his arms around himself. Dawson's gaze latched on to him, as if recognizing an oncoming meltdown. Without a word, Dawson closed his arms around Milo and stepped backward into the shower, pulling Milo beneath the hot water. He held Milo tightly against his chest while Milo shook.

Dawson's lips brushed Milo's ear. "It's all right, angel. Sometimes you have to destroy a few things to find out what's unbreakable. Now you know we can't be torn apart again. Everything else can be replaced."

Milo wasn't quite ready to stop falling apart yet. "I'm sorry you married a crazy person."

He felt more than heard Dawson's chuckle against his ear. "You're not, but I'm also not sorry. I'm pretty sure I'm the unbalanced one in this marriage. When I hold you like this, all my thoughts are completely insane. My brain starts churning out all these scenarios where I tear imaginary people apart for daring to think they'll take you from me. I get pretty dark and unstable, but you always stay."

Milo shrugged. "You're extra possessive because you love me and you have a reasonable fear of losing the people you love because your parents died young."

This time, Milo heard Dawson's laughter. Dawson blew out a sigh. "Why is it that you know exactly how to excuse my every fault, but you refuse to cut yourself any slack whatsoever?"

The tension drained from Milo's shoulders. Heat

finally penetrated his icy skin. Tears filled Milo's eyes unexpectedly. "I am so, *so* in love with you." Milo's voice cracked. "Let's disappear. I want to run away. Not because I'm ashamed, but because I want to be free. We deserve a quiet life. Let's liquidate everything and buy a place in the middle of nowhere. I can sell my paintings online only and no one would bother us again."

Dawson pressed his lips to Milo's temple. "Let's start with our honeymoon. Once we get settled away from everyone, we'll figure out our next move. Whatever it is, we'll be fine. I promise you we'll have a happy life and I'll be next to you the whole time."

As Dawson spoke, sounding loving and confident, Milo found his hands wandering. He stroked Dawson's back and sides before moving to squeeze his ass. His body stirred as their nude state and closeness began to override Milo's panic attack.

"There's baby oil on the shower caddy. I use it to make models look shiny during their poses. Get it. I want you to fuck me right here."

Dawson had been lightly stroking Milo's back, trying to keep him calm. His hands went still. Milo swore he stopped breathing. Milo half expected Dawson to deny him due to Milo's current mental state. Instead, Dawson did as told. He grabbed the baby oil. "Hands on the wall."

At the growled order, Milo immediately spun and flattened his palms against the shower wall. He knew Dawson's tone. Dawson's possessive side had come out to play.

Dawson urged Milo's hips back. Cool liquid ran down Milo's crack joining the hot water. Milo's eyes fell closed at the dueling sensations. He wanted to forget. Milo needed Dawson to wipe his mind clean of this horrible night for a little while. Dawson's finger slipped inside him. Milo widened his stance. A second finger joined the first. Dawson stretched. A loud pant burst from Milo. A third finger came into play as Dawson began pumping them in and out, mimicking sex. Milo's head dropped. He gasped for air. Dawson's fingers disappeared. Milo whimpered. The water stopped. Milo thought he might cry. He didn't want to stop, but he still started to straighten away from the wall. It was obvious Dawson didn't want to do this here. A sharp slap landed hard on his ass.

"Did I tell you to move?"

Milo immediately braced his hands on the wall again, resuming his earlier position. "No."

Dawson grunted, as if satisfied with Milo's

agreement. "Don't move from that spot." Dawson left him standing there, soaking wet and cold while he disappeared. A few long moments passed, but Milo never disobeyed. Suddenly, the hot water was back. A strange buzzing sound reverberated from the walls of the shower. Dawson gently turned Milo in his arms. His mouth came down hard on Milo's, sucking and biting Milo's lips until he did the same to Milo's tongue. He eased Milo toward the bench built into the shower wall. "I want you to ride the big boy while you suck my dick."

Milo sucked in a deep breath. The big boy was their ten-inch thrusting dildo that had looked much smaller online when they had ordered it. Neither of them had been willing to try it when it arrived, but it seemed Milo would be the first.

Dawson stroked Milo's aching cock. "You can take it. I've already lubed it for you." He looked turned on as hell. Milo couldn't say no. Even though Milo was certain he could not take it, he let Dawson walk him backward and ease him down. Milo didn't look away from Dawson's heated expression as Dawson held the toy in place and teased Milo's asshole with the tip. Milo sat. His breath left him as the toy moved inside him, hitting the spot that rolled his eyes back in his head. Even though he felt unnaturally full, he didn't back down. He held Dawson's stare as Dawson led Milo's mouth to his waiting dick. Milo made a show of licking him while fucking the toy. If Dawson wanted to watch, Milo would make sure he enjoyed himself.

With his feet planted, Milo rocked himself on the thrusting toy, letting it fuck him the way he liked. He played with Dawson's balls and bobbed on his dick, making Dawson moan. The louder Dawson got, the bolder Milo became. He shoved his hand between Dawson's legs and curled two fingers inside Dawson's asshole, leaving him no choice but to widen his stance and cling to the wall. He let Dawson abuse his throat, taking whatever he wanted as Milo's mind got distracted. The dildo in his ass did a hell of a job at massaging him internally, milking his prostate. Milo found himself riding the toy hard, taking his pleasure while Dawson fucked his mouth. Milo went wild, pounding his fingers inside Dawson's ass, trying to make him come hard. The spring inside Milo tightened by the second. He sucked Dawson's dick almost violently, as if he was sucking out his own cum. Milo's entire body jerked. An almost painful orgasm tore through him. Jets of cum splattered Dawson and the shower floor. Spasm after spasm rocked him as he slobbered all over

Dawson's dick. Dawson pulled his hair hard as he yanked Milo forward and shoved his cock down Milo's throat.

"Take it, Milo. Yes. Goddamn. You're amazing. Suck it." Hot cum filled Milo's mouth. He swallowed some, but mostly he let it drip from his chin while enjoying the way Dawson's cock twitched against his tongue. Dawson always made him feel powerful. Sucking Dawson's dick was sexy. The way Dawson stared at him filled Milo's chest with pride. Dawson pulled him up and into his arms. He sought Milo's mouth with his—like looking for his home. Time passed with no meaning as their tongues stroked and played. They had nowhere to be. They owed nothing to anyone except each other. Everything ceased to matter as they clung to each other. Dawson was right. They couldn't be broken. Everything outside of this was just noise. They would go on their honeymoon, but they wouldn't be running away. His mom could do her worst. Milo couldn't hear her anymore.

SEVEN

"WHAT ARE we going to do out here in the middle of nowhere for a week? I'm not complaining," Milo tacked on, making Dawson smile. "I'm just asking. Neither of us is accustomed to living in a tent for that long."

Dawson smirked. It was out of his control. "I'm sure I can keep us entertained." A laugh burst from Dawson as Milo's expression went through a series of hilarious changes. He looked thoughtful then intrigued, as if he could picture exactly what he wanted to try first. Finally, he rolled his eyes.

"Okay. We can't do that all the time."

An idea struck and Dawson pulled out his phone.

"No phones," Milo said, sounding defeated. "We said we would stay off our phones this week."

Dawson ignored him as he scrolled through his playlist and found a slow song. It reminded Dawson of all the ways he loved Milo. After turning up the volume as far as it would go, Dawson came to his feet and set the phone in his vacated camp chair.

He pulled Milo to his feet. "We won't get to dance together at our prom this year. I think about that a lot."

Milo pulled a sympathetic face as he let Dawson lure him into his embrace. "Me too, baby."

A lot of things bothered Dawson when it came to what they would miss. They would graduate together, but people would take pictures of them together in their caps and gown like they were brothers. Dawson wanted pictures of their love. They wouldn't get to wear matching tuxes and walk into prom holding hands. So much was being stolen from them, but this wasn't one of those things. They were taking a week out of time that belonged to them and no one else. No one would take these memories from them.

With Milo in his arms, Dawson matched the beat of the music. Milo swayed along. They fit. Everything about them went together perfectly.

Dawson's lips brushed the shell of Milo's ear as he sang along, letting Milo know this song was for him. Milo held him tighter. When the song ended, neither of them moved away. Dawson lips shifted lower, kissing the spot beneath Milo's ear. Love kept his feet frozen to the ground and his arms around Milo's waist.

"Someday, I'll give you my last name and you'll be free."

Milo nodded against Dawson's shoulder. "I believe."

Dawson knew he did, and that was why Dawson would never fail Milo. Milo's faith in him made Dawson feel like he could take over the world, except Dawson didn't want the world. He only wanted Milo. It was funny, though, the two things felt like they were the same. Owning Milo was exactly like being king of the whole world.

VALOR: **external link** I know you're leaving for your honeymoon today. You might want to stay longer than planned and accidentally on purpose leave Milo's phone behind.

A sense of dread rose inside Dawson as he clicked the link Valor had sent. He expected anything other than what he saw.

Rachel MacDermott arrested for allegedly

receiving and distributing child pornography.
Dawson blinked at the headline. He couldn't believe
what he was reading, but he knew he had to destroy
Milo's phone right that second. Not because he
thought Milo would rush to Rachel's defense, but
because reporters would likely start calling nonstop
any second. What Dawson wouldn't do was hide the
news from Milo.

Dawson rolled to his knees and straddled Milo's
body, pinning him to the bed. A sexy and sleepy
chuckle rumbled from Milo. He didn't open his eyes.
Dawson stole his chance to nuzzle and kiss Milo's
neck.

Milo brushed his fingers through Dawson's hair.
He felt so warm and sleep softened beneath Dawson
that Dawson almost forgot his reasons for waking
Milo. The small bed inside the camper was perfect
for them. Milo couldn't get away.

"What time is it?"

"Early," Dawson answered against Milo's
collarbone.

"Did you wake up needy?" Milo sounded more
asleep than awake.

Dawson snuggled as close as he could get and
held on. "I'm always needy, but I also need you to
turn your phone off."

127

Milo shifted slightly and kissed Dawson's ear. "It is off. No one ever calls me but you." He shrugged. "But I didn't want anyone interrupting our honeymoon."

"Good." Dawson kept his voice at barely a whisper, trying not to disturb Milo any more than necessary. "Go back to sleep."

For a moment, Dawson thought Milo had already drifted off again. Then Milo jerked a little, as if startling himself awake. "Is everything okay?" Milo asked, obviously trying to cling to the wisps of consciousness to keep up his end of the conversation.

"It is for us."

Milo wrapped his arms around Dawson and held on. "That's all I care about."

That was good. It was all Dawson cared about too. They had already done their time playing by other people's rules—like puppets on strings. Now they were parked in the middle of the woods with nothing but each other and time. Eventually, Milo would wake, and Dawson would have to tell him that his mom was some kind of creepy pervert, which was a new low. Still, she couldn't touch them. In fact, it sounded like she had bigger problems with her reputation than her son marrying someone she thought below them. Dawson imagined they would be the least of her problems for a very long time.

Dawson's eyelids grew heavy. After making love for hours, Dawson had driven a few hours through the night until they were hidden away in the mountains. Now Dawson was exhausted. Being in Milo's arms made his body feel heavy—like he was safe at home. It was their time now. No one could tear them apart.

Keep an eye out for the next Candied Crush, *Beautifully Blue.*

ABOUT THE AUTHOR

Charity Parkerson is an award-winning and multi-published author with several companies. Born with no filter from her brain to her mouth, she decided to take this odd quirk and insert it in her characters.

*Eight-time Readers' Favorite Award Winner
   *2015 Passionate Plume Award Finalist
   *2013 Reviewers' Choice Award Winner
   *2012 ARRA Finalist for Favorite Paranormal Romance
   *Five-time winner of The Mistress of the Darkpath

Connect with her online:

—Sign up for my newsletter: http://bit.ly/CharityNews
   —Join my readers' group on Facebook: http://bit.ly/CharitysTribe
   —Website: charityparkerson.com

—Facebook:
facebook.com/authorCharityParkerson
facebook.com/TheMenofSin
—Twitter: twitter.com/CharityParkerso
—Instagram: Instagram.com/sinnerauthor